CW00810883

SPECIAL MESSAGE TO READERS

This book is published by

THE ULVERSCROFT FOUNDATION,

a registered charity in the U.K., No. 264873

The Foundation was established in 1974 to provide funds to help towards research, diagnosis and treatment of eye diseases. Below are a few examples of contributions made by THE ULVERSCROFT FOUNDATION:

★ A new Children's Assessment Unit at Moorfield's Hospital, London.

★ Twin operating theatres at the Western Ophthalmic Hospital, London.

★ The Frederick Thorpe Ulverscroft Chair of Ophthalmology at the University of Leicester.

★ Eye Laser equipment to various eye hospitals.

If you would like to help further the work of the Foundation by making a donation or leaving a legacy, every contribution, no matter how small, is received with gratitude. Please write for details to:

THE ULVERSCROFT FOUNDATION,
The Green, Bradgate Road, Anstey,
Leicestershire, LE7 7FU. England.

Telephone: (0533) 364325

AUTUMN OF DECEPTION

To escape seduction by her employer's son, Charles—an officer recently returned from the battle of Waterloo, Mary Dordon, governess to his stepsisters, is forced to return home. At first Mary is happy to be back in the sheltered environment of her home. Then she discovers that two local girls have recently been murdered—both in bizarre circumstances. At the home of the local squire, to her astonishment, she meets Charles, and a few days later one of the mill hands is found strangled. Who is the insane killer in their midst?

MAUREEN STEPHENSON

AUTUMN OF DECEPTION

Complete and Unabridged

LINFORD
Leicester

First published in Great Britain in 1982 by
Robert Hale Ltd.,
London

First Linford Edition
published June 1989

British Library CIP Data

Stephenson, Maureen
Autumn of deception.—Large print ed.—
Linford romance library
I. Title
823′.914[F]

ISBN 0-7089-6694-2

Published by
F. A. Thorpe (Publishing) Ltd.
Anstey, Leicestershire

Set by Rowland Phototypesetting Ltd.
Bury St. Edmunds, Suffolk
Printed and bound in Great Britain by
T. J. Press (Padstow) Ltd., Padstow, Cornwall

1

I TURNED the key in the lock. There was a quiet click. Then undressing as quickly as I could, I climbed into bed, and lay there between the smooth sheets in the still darkness, a pulse beating in my head, my heart thumping in my breast.

I was safe now, but I must try to keep calm. Sleep, I told myself, decide tomorrow what to do. And mercifully the tumult within me started to lessen, my eyelids began to droop, and soon I was drifting in a misty world of half-formed dreams.

Suddenly there was a knock at the door! Instantly I was awake; all my senses alert. I had felt this might happen. Somewhere far away a church clock chimed the hour, and when it finished the silence in the room hung heavy and oppressive. I held my breath and waited. Then the knocking came again, this time even bolder. A tremor ran through me as I sat up, my mouth dry as ashes.

"Who is it?" I whispered, even though I knew who it was.

"It's me, Charles. Open the door, Mary. I want to talk to you."

I did not move.

"Please, Mary." There was now an urgent tone in his voice. "Just for a few minutes."

"Go away," I whispered frantically.

"Please, Mary."

His voice now sounded full of pain.

"Leave me in peace. I beg of you."

Then I lay back, and buried my face in the pillows. All I could see was a deep darkness, my heart fluttering like a bird.

Open that door and my respectability would end.

"Mary, you have no call to treat me in this fashion."

Then I heard him walk away, and the agony was over. I turned over on my back and stared into the darkness, my thoughts a troubled sea. Almost a year now since I had taken up the post of governess to

Charles' young step-sisters, Cathy and Jane. Their father, Joshua Field, was a wealthy Birmingham gun manufacturer, whose fortune had been further increased by selling arms to the British Army in the recent war against Napoleon.

I taught the usual subjects refined young girls were taught, but above all the pianoforte. Not that their mother was a music-lover, but she considered the playing of this instrument an essential social accomplishment which would help her daughters to secure husbands.

Cathy and Jane were friendly, intelligent girls, and made good progress. Mrs. Field was pleased, and I was contented. Then just over a week ago Charles arrived home on leave from Paris, and everything changed.

I can see him now, the night he arrived, standing in the hall, embracing the family, whilst I stood at a respectful distance watching.

His father and stepmother were so proud of him. They had reason to be. He was a captain in the Royal Horse Artillery and had recently fought under Wellington at Waterloo. He was a tall, dark, impressive-looking man in his blue jacket faced with scarlet, gold lacing across the chest, his long fur-lined cloak, his half-moon sabre at his side. He was given a hero's welcome.

Mr. Field gave instructions for champagne to be opened, and I watched Charles take off his cloak and hand it to a servant. There was weariness in his face, lines of fatigue about his mouth. Then suddenly he had turned, and looked at me, and his look had been so penetrating I had lowered my eyes.

"I haven't seen you before?" he had enquired in a pleasant manner.

"This is Miss Dordon, our governess," young Cathy had said, holding onto his arm.

"I don't like girls with red hair."

"He doesn't mean it," laughed Cathy. "He always teases."

I had gone up to my room after that—it was, after all, a family reunion.

The next day whilst giving Cathy and

Jane their pianoforte lesson, he had come into the room and stood by the window listening. When the lesson finished, he walked across and leaned on the instrument, staring at me in a manner I found most disconcerting.

"Run and play in the garden, girls. I'll call you when lunch is ready."

The two girls ran off, glad of a brief respite.

"I had no idea you played the pianoforte. Where did you learn?"

I started tidying up a pile of books.

"Miss Digbeth's Academy."

"She has a good reputation. I must say, you're very patient with those two."

"Oh, they're good girls, and making excellent progress."

He remained watching my every movement. I started making notes for the afternoon's work, feeling self-conscious, and wondering when he would go.

"Have they all got red hair in your family?" he enquired at length.

I could not help smiling.

"No. Just me. But they tell me my

grandfather had red hair too. It's a pity you don't like it, but I can't do anything about it."

"Oh, but I do like it. Didn't Cathy tell you I tease?"

He started thumbing through the Beethoven book. Meanwhile I finished making my notes, and prepared to go.

"I'd be very pleased if you would play something for me," he said, handing me the book.

Surprised and flattered at his interest, I opened it.

"Would you like 'Für Elise'?"

"I would like it very much."

I sat down and played. When I finished, I looked up and found him regarding me in a thoughtful manner.

"You know, you're a surprising governess. You're good enough to play at the charity concerts at the town hall."

"You're very kind. Do you play the pianoforte?"

"Yes, but I prefer the violin. Actually I've been experimenting with composition. There was so little to do before

Waterloo. For a whole month I was in Brussels billeted with a family in Grand Place. Charming people. They had a pianoforte and allowed me to play it. To while away the time I composed a sonata for pianoforte and violin. It's not very good. Needs a good deal of improvement. Would you like to try it out with me?"

Intrigued, I agreed, and he went up to his room, returning a few minutes later with his violin and the music manuscript. We played it through, stopping every now and then to make alterations. Lunch was forgotten. We played it through a second time, and then a third. I liked the melody Charles had woven into the composition. It had both charm and style.

"It's coming, Mary," he said enthusiastically. "I may of course call you Mary."

I really did not know what to make of him. He was the most unlikely soldier I had ever met.

"What's the matter? You look troubled."

"It isn't usual to meet a soldier who

composes sonatas in his spare time. May I ask what you will do now that the war is over?"

"I'm not sure, but I know I won't be a gun manufacturer like my father."

And so began our friendship, at least it was for me. He started accompanying us on our daily walks. I liked him. He had a relaxed manner that made it easy to talk to him, and so early in the week I found myself telling him I thought his sonata so good it ought to be published and publicly performed.

"Do you really think so!" he exclaimed, obviously delighted. "It will have to have a title of course. I think I'll call it 'The Brussels Sonata'."

That evening I helped him write out the score for the publisher, working till well past midnight, and the following morning Charles went into Birmingham and posted it.

And so the week had passed. I considered Charles' interest in me to be purely musical, and when he returned to his regiment I doubted if I would ever see him again. There was a possibility of Mr. Field opening a factory in India in the near future, and when this happened, Mrs. Field, Cathy and Jane would accompany him, and my services would be terminated.

But tonight everything had changed. Mr. Field and Charles had gone out—a meeting, I think, in connection with the factory, and I had spent the evening sewing with Mrs. Field in her private sitting-room. She was a woman of a nervous disposition and never cared to spend the evening alone. She was embroidering a bed-cover, a beautiful piece of work, whilst I had the mundane task of hemming yards and yards of cambric for the servants' new gowns. Nevertheless it was a comparatively pleasant evening, and at half-past ten Mrs. Field retired for bed.

I was just considering going myself when I remembered I had left my shawl in the music-room. I crossed the hall and entered the room, where, to my surprise, Charles was standing before the fire. I remember not liking the curiously intense expression on his face as he looked at me.

"Charles, I had no idea you were here," I exclaimed. "I thought you were still at the meeting."

"I left early."

"I just came in to look for my shawl."

And as I passed him, suddenly, without any warning, his arms were around me, and he was kissing me in such a hard, hungry manner on the mouth, pressing his body close to mine, my legs shook beneath me. I managed to pull away.

"I've been wanting to do that all week."

He spoke in such a smug, satisfied tone, rarely have I felt so angry. I slapped his face and ran from the room.

Sleep was now impossible.

I sat up in bed, thinking sadly it was a familiar story. The son of the house becoming enamoured of a servant, although in my case I was a little above a servant. They were hole-in-the-corner affairs, sordid and secret, and when discovered the girl was dismissed.

Then suddenly I was angry. He would not dare to behave like that if I was a woman of his own class, but a governess was an easy target, alone and vulnerable. They always have their fun with lower-class women, then marry one of their own kind, my Aunt Grace used to say. She was housekeeper at Golding Castle, and well acquainted with the habits of wealthy young gentlemen.

I was filled with a sense of disillusionment, and annoyance at my unrealistic attitude to life. What a fool I had been. Men like Charles Field did not have platonic friendships with women. It was quite obvious his aim was to seduce me.

There was no alternative but to return home. Home! Suddenly I longed for its security with a fierceness that made me feel weak. I would go in the morning, and leave a letter for Mrs. Field.

I think I must have dozed off, for when I awoke the room was filled with the pale light of dawn. It was chilly. I rose hurriedly, shivering, and dressed. There was no time to lose, and quickly packing my few belongings as silently as I could into the old straw bag father had given to me, I put on my poke bonnet, and with nervous fingers tied the ribbon under my chin. All I had to do now was write the letter to Mrs. Field. This I found very difficult. In the end I wrote the following:

31st October 1815.

Dear Mrs. Field,

It is with deep regret that I have to inform you I must return home immediately. Forgive me but I cannot give an explanation for this extra-ordinary behaviour. Do not judge me too harshly. I shall think of you with gratitude.

Give my love to Cathy and Jane, and tell them I shall sadly miss them. My heartfelt thanks to you and Mr. Field for all your kindnesses to me.

Again I ask for your forgiveness.

Your humble servant,
Mary Dordon.

Propping the letter up on the bedside

table, the maid would see it when she came in to clean the room, I unlocked the door with trembling fingers and peered out.

It was still dark in the corridor outside, the only window being of dark-stained glass. Picking up my straw bag I gently closed the door and tiptoed down the silent corridor. Then down the wide carpeted stairs, my hand on the polished mahogany rail, my heart thumping against my ribs. In another hour the servants would be up.

The last stair creaked. I paused and waited. Not a sound came from upstairs.

I was now impatient to be out of the house, and crossing the kitchen hastily my foot knocked against a stool, and it went over with a clatter on the stone floor. The noise seemed deafening. It was sure to waken someone. I stood still, holding my breath. But to my surprise the house slept on.

Now to slide back the great bolt on the kitchen door. I found it heavy and stiff, but pushing with all my strength at last it opened, and I was out of the house, in the dawn light of a new day, hurrying down the back drive, then down the road to Birmingham.

Men and women on their way to work gave me curious glances. I walked quickly, heeding no one, and within half an hour I was at the Golden Cross Inn. Birmingham at that early hour was already crowded, the roads conjested with covered waggons bringing goods into the town, and carts ladened with farm produce for the early market.

As I boarded the Leicester Flyer and settled in a corner seat I was filled with a sense of emptiness. I had been deceived, and it hurt.

The driver blew his horn, and we set off through the noisy crowded streets, the air filled with smoke and grime. The day was unreal; the pattern broken. I sat in the corner and dozed.

When I awoke the scenery had changed and we were out in the open countryside. Someone had opened the window, and the air was fresh and clean. The sun came out, shining on lush meadowlands and woods, on timber-framed farm houses by placidly flowing rivers. Soothing and timeless, and my mental anguish began to subside.

As I listened to my fellow passengers, mainly country people discussing country matters, solid honest folk, I found myself thinking of my father. He had begged me not to take the post in Birmingham, but being impulsive and strong-willed I had gone.

And why? Because I did not want to marry Mr. Hastilow. I had wondered a great deal about this, and in the end decided, in my case, it was because I had been educated, which had made me dissatisfied. Normally girls of my class were ignored. A dame school for a few years was considered sufficient.

It was all due to Mother's intervention. Her family kept an inn at Stratford-on-Avon. Not one of the big important places, but a modest establishment down a side-street. But they were admirable, hard-working people, whose aim was to better themselves. Mother's sister, Esther, had done that. She had been a pretty girl, and lucky enough to receive a reasonable education, and had married a lawyer. Mother was convinced it was Esther's educated mind that had achieved the proposal, so before she had died she had extracted a promise from Father that I too should be educated, in order that I should attain the exalted status of Aunt Esther.

So at the age of ten I had been sent off to Miss Digbeth's Academy—Miss Digbeth's being considered the best in the Midlands. She was also a good musician, giving instruction on the harpsichord, flute and pianoforte. I had chosen the pianoforte, never considering the fact that father could never afford to buy one, and would have been pleased if I had chosen the flute. But that was a long time ago.

My brother Harry had been sent to a boys' school in Coventry the previous year. I missed Mother, and him, very much, so altogether I was glad to start a new life.

And so the years had passed and we had grown up, the three of us meeting in the holidays. Then Harry had joined the Navy, which was quite an extraordinary thing to do considering we lived in the centre of England, and you cannot get further from the sea than that.

After I left school everyone expected me to marry Mr. Hastilow. He was suitable from a financial point of view, being the most prosperous farmer in the district. He was also a widower, elderly—at least forty. Not that I objected to his age. Lucy Harborough had married a man of forty and she was very happy. No, I feel age does not come into these matters. The truth was I considered him a cold man with no sense of humour.

The matter had come to a head when he had given a little party and invited me. He proposed during the evening, and I turned him down as graciously as I could.

He was not perturbed by my refusal. Indeed, he said he had expected it and would continue to propose until I changed my mind. He was a very determined man.

Aunt Grace said I was a fool. I would never get a better offer. What did it matter that I did not love him. I would never do a day's housework in my life, and be the best-dressed woman in Golding Magna. Father could not understand what all the fuss was about.

I knew I was trapped. I would end up married to him, mistress of that dark house up the lane with its torpid atmosphere, and that I did not want.

I had decided I would have to leave the district. With the help of Miss Digbeth I had acquired the post of governess to the Field girls. It had been hard in the beginning. Homesickness had been the worst. But being young, I had soon adapted myself to the new life.

Now I felt defeated.

"We could do with a drop of rain." The voice of the elderly man opposite broke into my thoughts. "Land's as dry as a bone."

To my pleasant surprise we were now travelling through familiar country. Shustoke, Over Whitacre, Appleby Parva.

When the coach stopped at the turnpike gate at Gospel Oak I alighted. It was a tiny place consisting of the turnpike cottage and three silk-weavers' cottages. Away on the far horizon were the blue hills of Shropshire.

The driver handed me my bag.

"Nice change from Brummagem," he remarked, looking around.

I eagerly agreed with him. Then with a cheery wave and a smart crack of his whip he moved off. I stood watching the coach until it disappeared round the bend in a cloud of dust. I felt a chapter of my life had closed. Mr. Dagley, the turnpike keeper, closed the gate and regarded me with surprise.

"Good afternoon, Mr. Dagley," I called.

"Hello, Mary, didn't expect to see you until Christmas."

Giving him a quick smile and a wave, and before he could ask any questions, I set off down the little lane that turned off the turnpike.

It was quiet in the lane. Evening of a

sunny day, and I felt a deep contentment. The blackthorn hedge grew thick and high on each side, its branches heavy with purple sloes, and bryony hung on the blackthorn like necklaces of orange beads. Ahead of me a pair of pheasants with their distinctive colouring crossed the lane and disappeared in the hedge. Of course this was the pheasant season, and Father had the right to shoot one if it settled on our land. I wondered if Effie was cooking one for supper. The thought of it made me feel hungry.

Passing Mr. Hastilow's farm I wondered momentarily at his reaction when we would eventually meet. Would there be embarrassment? Then I smiled to myself. He had probably got himself a bride and forgotten all about me.

When I reached the pond I was nearly home. Through the pale gold sedge the water lay still and dark. I paused a moment, remembering the cold winters when I had skated on it with Harry. I was very fond of Harry, and found myself wondering if I would ever see him again.

As I continued along the lane, swinging the old straw bag at my side, the air filled with bird-song and sunshine, I had no inkling of the drama that lay ahead.

The lane now started to dip. Ancient oaks and ashes grew on each side, their branches intertwining overhead so that one could only see small patches of the sky.

I first heard the sound of rushing water, and the thudding of the wheel, then through a gap in the trees I saw it, nestling in the little valley below—Golding Mill, on the banks of the Bourne. The evening sunshine warming the old red Tudor brick, and the water on the wheel-floats giving a final glitter before plunging into the tail-race in lacy patterns of white foam.

Beyond lay the red brick byre, the stables, and the cart-house. Solid and secure. I should never have left it.

I started to run.

2

I STEPPED into the porch. Nothing had changed. The swallows as usual had spent the summer here, and all that remained was their empty nest above the door, and wisps of straw and dead grass lay upon the floor.

The front door was slightly ajar. I pushed it open and peeped into the parlour, but to my disappointment no one was there. Then I remembered, at this time of day, father would be up at the mill-pond.

Leaving my bag in the porch, I walked along the brick path through the little garden that lay before the mill, a sweet confusion of the last of summer's herbs and flowers. Then across the footbridge that spanned the tail-race, and as I climbed the old stone steps by the side of the wheel I saw him, standing by the sluice-gate.

The roar from the mill-race was so loud, if I had shouted, he would not have heard. So pausing at the top of the steps, I watched him bend down and close the gate. The roar from the water ceased, and the wheel gradually came to a creaking halt, the floats still dripping. Then he turned and saw me.

"Father!" I cried, and ran the few yards to him.

I always felt such a rush of warmth at the sight of him. A big man, with a dishevelled head of grey hair, bushy side-whiskers, and such a loud voice, sometimes he frightened Effie, our housekeeper. But as I drew near, I saw he had aged since last we met. There were new lines upon his face, and he was much thinner.

"Mary!"

He embraced me warmly and kissed me on the cheek.

"Father, you've had the fever again."

He nodded.

"It was at the end of the summer, but

I'm right as rain now. Must admit it was the worst bout I've had."

"But why didn't you tell me?"

"There was no point in worrying you."

He did not want me to know, I thought, as we walked along the bank of the mill-pond to the overflow. He would regard his illness as a weakness to be fought, and he did not want me to see him fight his battles.

"Have you forgiven me?"

"Forgiven you for what?"

"Going off to Birmingham."

"Of course I have. But why didn't you tell me you were coming? I didn't expect you until Christmas. Something wrong?"

"No," I lied, speaking in a forced light voice and looking away. But I had forgotten Father always knew when I was not telling the truth.

"I think life's bruised you a bit, Mary," he commented as he bent down to inspect the overflow. "And if there's a man in it, I'll horsewhip him."

In silence we retraced our steps round the mill-pond, but when we reached the top of the mill-race steps, I could control my feelings no longer, and all the misery I had experienced in the last twenty-four hours suddenly burst into a fit of weeping.

Father sat down on the steps, and I leaned my head against his great chest like I did when I was a child. When my weeping subsided he spoke.

"When you were little, Mary, you and Harry went off to school. I had to put up with it as best I could. At the time I felt your mother knew best. Now I'm not so sure. I think it would have been better if you had stayed at home with me. And Harry, I wasn't really surprised when he went off and joined the Navy. Such an adventurous boy, he was never interested in milling. But when you went, I never expected that, and I thought, I've lost Mary now. She'll never come back, and that's what education's done for her. But I was wrong, you have come back. Now dry your tears and answer me one last question. Have you been a good girl?"

"Oh yes, Father," I replied earnestly.

"Well, what are you crying for?"

We entered the parlour, familiar and cosy. The walls needed white-washing. I could never remember a time when they did not, Father was always careless about such matters, but the furniture arranged about the room was of a quality any prosperous miller would possess, handed down from one generation to the next.

There was the circular gate-legged table in dark oak, with the high-back carved chairs, the settle and the dresser. Here the family treasures were displayed. On the top shelf were the pewter tankards and plates, these were very old and never touched; the next two shelves were filled with the best blue china, only used when visitors called; on the bottom shelf were stacked the family Bible, hymn books, and a battered edition of *The Treatment of Diseases in Cows And Sheep*, for the property was both mill and farm.

Hanging on the wall to the left of the dresser was a framed tapestry map of Warwickshire, and on the wall between the window and the door hung the

Cromwell clock with its brass face, one hand, and heavy pendulum swinging on a chain. That was the most prized of Father's possessions, and had belonged to a Puritan ancestor.

There was a fire burning brightly in the ingle-nook, and resting across the top was a great oak beam, full of cracks. Ship's timber, father always told us. It had been over our ingle-nook three hundred years, which meant that when the young Henry the eighth had been on the throne it had been part of a ship sailing against the French. Father was proud of that timber and always talking about it. I used to wonder if it had influenced Harry in his decision to join the Navy. Whatever it was, he had gone, that bright summer's morning two years ago.

"Any news from Harry?" I asked, untying my bonnet.

"Not a word since the spring. I've been getting a bit worried about him. Anyway, come into the mill. I've been doing a bit of reorganising."

He opened the door that led into the

mill section of the house. I followed him, always delighted when Father wished to discuss the running of the mill with me.

The machinery now lay motionless and silent, waiting for tomorrow, and everywhere was covered in a fine dust of flour. It lay on the windows, the floor, on the ladder at the end of the room, the machinery, and even clung to the cobwebs, and over all there pervaded its delicate odour. This room was the weighing-room. Here the sacks of flour were weighed to make sure they held the correct amount before delivery.

A stout young man with a round boyish face dressed in a smock was securing a sack of grain to the hoist in readiness for tomorrow. He stopped working as we approached and gave me a big grin.

"Hello, Mary, fancy seeing you," he exclaimed. "Are you home for good?"

"I think so, Hopper. How's everything?"

"Fine!"

He gave me another big grin. He was always cheerful, and this was no mean feat considering the anguish he must suffer from his unrequited love of Rose, our dairy-maid.

"I'm not having any sacks stored on the ground floor in future," said Father. "Some days we can't move in here. Everything goes up to the second and third floors."

The mill cat, a friendly young tabby, walked up and rubbed her body against my legs, purring. As I bent down to stroke her, footsteps on the ladder at the end of the room caused me to look up. To my surprise a strange young man with a pale, sensitive face was descending the ladder.

"Oh, Mary, this is Hugh. Hugh Morganwy," introduced father. "He's been with us since the summer. I don't know what I would have done without him when I was ill."

Hugh gave a friendly smile and walked across to meet me with a confident self-assured manner. As he took my hand I noticed an odd-looking gold ring on his finger engraved with the letters "CM".

"I'm very pleased to meet you, Mary. Your father has often spoken about you."

He spoke English like someone speaking a foreign language, pronouncing each word carefully in a musical, lilting way. Where had I heard such a voice before? Suddenly I remembered the voice of a Cardiff girl at Miss Digbeth's.

"What a surprise to meet a Welshman!"

"I don't see why it should be such a surprise."

"I'm sorry, I've met so few Welsh people. Which part are you from?"

"The Black Mountains. Do you know them?"

"I've never been to Wales."

"Ah, more's the pity, and Wales' loss."

He gave me a warm smile of appraisal. He was a flatterer.

"I'll be going now, Mr. Dordon," called Hopper at the door. "Good night, Mary. Nice to see you back."

"Thanks, Hopper. Good night."

Hopper closed the door, and Hugh Morganwy took off his smock.

"I've rented a little cottage at Nether Asterley," he said, looking rather pointedly at me. "I'd be honoured if you and Mr. Dordon would care to come along one evening. Gets a bit lonely sometimes, not knowing anybody."

"We'd be glad to, Hugh," replied Father. "Any time. Everything all right for the morning? Castle barley comes first thing."

"Don't you worry, Mr. Dordon. Everything's taken care of. I'll be off now. Good night, Mary. Good night, Mr. Dordon."

And with a cheerful smile, he opened the outside door and disappeared from view.

"What a pleasant man," I exclaimed as we walked back into the parlour.

"Believe it or not, besides being a good mill-hand, he's a poet and singer as well." Father spoke with pride in his voice. "And what's more, he was good to me when I was ill. Looked after me as if I was a child."

Father sat down on the settle.

"He's learnt the job quickly too," he said, lighting his evening pipe. "Never been in a mill before."

I went to the kitchen to find Effie. I had been right. She was in the act of taking a pheasant off the spit, and the room was filled with its delicious aroma.

"Mary!" she exclaimed, her eyes lighting up behind her steel-rimmed spectacles. She placed the bird carefully on a large plate on the table, then gave me a big hug.

I was very fond of Effie. Her real name was Euphemia. She had been the only child of an impoverished country parson. Her mother had died when she was born, and on her father's death, finding herself penniless and homeless, had been forced to offer her housekeeping services at the Mop Fair at Stratford-on-Avon.

I remember going with Father, and seeing the waggoners standing in line with their piece of whipcord, the shepherds with their wool, the house-servants with their mops and rolling-pins, and I, the motherless child, had been drawn to the motherly woman with the gentle face and grey locks.

"I knew you were back. I saw your bag in the porch. Oh, it is good to see you, Mary." And her eyes filled with tears. Effie cried easily, but none the less they were sincere. "I have missed you. But I thought you weren't coming home till Christmas."

"I've decided to change my job."

Effie frowned.

"I thought you liked it there. Playing the pianoforte every day. You know how you missed playing when you were at home. And all those fancy shops in Birmingham! I expect you were homesick."

She turned her attention to the pheasant and pushed a fork into it. The juices bubbled out.

"I thought it would be pheasant," I said, watching her.

"Not a word about this one," she laughed. "Your father shot it in the lane."

No one was allowed to shoot game in the lane. It was regarded as the property of Sir Francis Drew, the local squire, but as Father said it takes a strong man to resist a sitting bird.

"How have you been keeping, Effie?"

She put a cover over the bird and set it down in the hearth.

"I've been keeping quite well considering."

Then she sat down in the rocking chair, and gently rocked herself. There was silence. She obviously wanted to tell me something and found it difficult to start.

"Considering what?"

"I do get tired these days, Mary, turning that spit's back-breaking. I suppose it's old age. I would like one of those new cast-iron ranges with a big oven, and there's a place that heats water too. They've got two at Golding Castle," she added enviously.

"Why don't you ask Father to buy one?"

"I don't like asking."

Effie's timid voice trailed off.

"I'll ask him."

"Oh, would you really, Mary? Thank you. You're so kind."

She leaned forward and tested the potatoes bubbling in the pot over the fire.

"I've just met the new man," I said, sitting on the stool beside her. "Hugh Morganwy."

"Oh, isn't he nice! I do like Hugh, and it's so comical how he came to start here." Effie smiled. "It was the day a pig got out. Christmas Boultbee says he can't understand it because he remembers closing the sty gate. Personally I think Christmas had had a drop too much that day. Anyway, this pig walked into the house, and the cellar door was open. Well, you know what inquisitive creatures they are—down it went. What a noise it made.

"I lit a lantern and went down, and I couldn't get it out. So I went into the weighing-room for help, and there was this Welshman come to buy some flour. He said to me, 'I'm very good at getting pigs out of cellars,' and he came and helped me. What a time we had. Anyway, after we put the pig back in the sty, we got talking—him, your father, and me, and it ended up with Hugh asking your father for a job, and he started the next day. Your father's so pleased with him. When your father was ill he ran the place like clockwork."

"Effie, I wish you had written to me when Father was ill. I would have come home straight away."

"He wouldn't let me. He said I'm not having Mary worrying for nothing—nothing, that's the way he regarded it."

"How's Christmas?"

"Drunk as usual. It's a wonder any animals get fed, any field ploughed. I don't know why your father keeps him on."

"And Rose?"

Besides being our dairy-maid, Rose was Christmas Boultbee's daughter.

"Rose is all right. One of these days there'll be wedding-bells for Rose and Hopper. Just you see I'm right."

Effie rose to her feet.

"I'd best be getting on. Your father will

be wanting his supper, and you'll be wanting a bite to eat."

"I'll take my bag upstairs and have a quick wash."

"Danny's already taken it up, and I told him to put some water in your jug."

I walked slowly up the narrow polished stairs, past the little window where the statue of the Indian goddess stood on the sill, a present from Harry on his leave. At the top of the stairs ran a narrow corridor, and directly ahead up two further steps was a shabby brown door. This was the grinding-room. I opened the door and peeped in.

Encased in a wooden covering were the great millstones in the centre of the room. There was a trapdoor in the floor near by, and another in the ceiling with a chain-pulley connecting. This brought up sacks of grain or flour from the ground floor, and at the far end was the ladder which led down to the weighing-room. Sacks of flour awaiting delivery or collection were leaning against a wall.

I closed the door. Father's work never

ceased. There was always plenty of grain to grind in Warwickshire. Father's bedroom was next to the grinding-room, and the door was open. As I approached there were sounds of movement from within. Knowing Father and Effie to be downstairs, I pushed the door open further, and to my astonishment found Danny standing with his back to me at Father's chest of drawers.

"Danny, what are you doing in here?" I exclaimed, feeling a little annoyed.

Danny spun round, his hands behind his back—a great hulk of a fellow, with a body as strong as an ox, and the mind of a child. For this reason Father employed him to carry the heavy sacks to and from the carts—the mill not having an outside hoist. It was more out of pity for his widowed mother, for he needed constant supervision. He now stood before me, his smock torn and dirty as usual, his toes showing through his broken boots.

"Why are your hands behind your back, Danny?"

"I ain't hiding anything. I ain't got nothing."

There was a distinctly guilty expression on his face.

"Danny, you're not telling the truth. Open your hand."

He made no move.

"If you show me what you have, I'll tell Effie to give you a piece of cake."

"Promise?"

"I promise."

The thought of the cake did it, and he opened his hand. Nestling in his great palm was Father's mother-of-pearl snuff-box. He handed it over reluctantly, and I placed it on top of the chest of drawers with the others. There was one of tortoise-shell and one of ivory. They had been left to Father by Grandfather Dordon, and he prized them highly.

"Danny, you know Father does not like anyone to come in his room. All Effie said was to bring up my bag and put water in the jug. Have you done it?"

"Yes, Mary. But Mr. Dordon's got such pretty things." And a big smile lit up his childlike face. "I was only playing with them."

"You must not come in here again," I said firmly. "If you do I shall have to tell Father and he'll be angry."

To my astonishment he clenched his fists and moved menacingly towards me. For a moment I thought he was going to strike me.

"You do that, Mary, and he won't let me work here any more. I like working here."

I had never seen him in such an angry mood. Usually he was obedient, and situations were comparatively easy to handle. Just then Effie's voice sounded from below, and the tension eased.

"Danny, you're a long time taking Mary's bag upstairs."

"I'm coming down, Effie," he called back, moving towards the door. "And Mary says I can have a piece of cake." Then he turned round. "You're not angry with me any more, Mary?"

"No, of course not." I smiled.

He left the room and hurried down the

stairs. The storm over I breathed a sigh of relief and hurried down the corridor. One of these days Danny was going to get into serious trouble.

Opening the door of my room, I stepped inside, and a feeling of nostaglia swept through me. The same four-poster with its white linen cover embroidered with red roses and blue corn-flowers. I never failed to admire my grandmother's needlework. I had never known her, for she had died before I was born.

On the mantel over the fireplace were the little china shepherd and shepherdess that had belonged to my mother, painted in such delicate shades of greens and blues; my fingers touched them lovingly. At the window the same curtains with the faded yellow roses.

It was only me that had changed.

In the fading light I quickly washed my hands and face, smoothed my hair in the mirror, and hurried from the room.

As I walked into the parlour Effie was setting out the supper dishes on the table, whilst Father was carving the pheasant.

I took my usual place opposite the window, and looked across onto the western slope of the valley, the top of which cut a clean line against the sky, and on the horizon to the south-west was the black cloud of Golding Wood—one of the last remnants of the Forest of Arden.

"Golding Wood looks almost sinister in the twilight," I remarked casually.

I saw the look Effie gave Father.

She took her place opposite him. We are an informal household, and Effie regarded as a member of the family. Now I am very sensitive to atmospheres, and there was something wrong. The meal continued with Father making a little joke about Sir Francis as we ate the pheasant.

"What are your plans now, Mary?" asked Father when we had finished eating. "Now that you've tested freedom earning your own living, are you going to get another governess post? You know I would like it best if you stayed here."

I gave a rueful smile.

"I'm not sure what to do, Father."

"Why don't you have a talk with your Aunt Grace?"

"That's a good idea. I'll go tomorrow."

Effie complained of tiredness and went up to her room, and I took the dishes to the kitchen and washed them. Actually I had not given my future any thought at all, and now that I thought of it I was not sure I wanted to be a governess again. What could I do?

I returned to the parlour. Father was whittling at a piece of wood.

"What's this one going to be?"

He looked up and smiled.

"It's going to be a swallow in flight. What's the matter with Effie, going to bed so early?"

"She tells me she gets very tired these days. Father, she would like one of those new cast-iron ranges. It would make life a bit easier for her."

Father looked up puzzled.

"She can have one," he shouted in an exasperated tone. "Why doesn't she ask me herself?"

"She finds you a bit intimidating, father."

"Intimidating?" he exclaimed, still shouting. "Why ever should she think that?"

I kissed him on the forehead.

"It's the shouting," I said softly. "I'm going to bed."

"Oh, Mary, before you go, I've been thinking about your last letter Effie read to me—one of these days I'll have to get myself a pair of spectacles—and I seem to remember you saying a soldier son was coming on leave. He's the reason why you ran away. Am I right?"

I took a deep breath.

"Yes, Father."

"You did well. But I'll tell you this." And he clenched his fist. "If he sets foot across my threshold—"

"It's all over. I will never see him again. Good night, Father."

I went upstairs to my room, my mind filled with pain. Forget him, I told myself. Forget you ever met him.

I climbed into bed and lay there

listening to the soothing sound of the Bourne falling over a lip of rock on the other side of the lane. I started to feel better. I had come home, and that was all that mattered, but just as I was about to doze off I found myself thinking of the look Effie had given Father when I had mentioned the wood.

3

I AWOKE to the familiar sounds of the mill—a continuous thumping and creaking, with the occasional rattle of the chain-hoist, and from outside came the muffled roar of the mill-race. To me it was a harmonious sound, for it spelled peace and security. It was home.

A wagon drew up outside. There were footsteps, Hugh's lilting voice, then the gruff voice of Will Sheepy, the castle waggoner. Suddenly I remembered I was going to Golding Castle today, and full of eager anticipation—I always enjoyed a visit to Aunt Grace—I got out of bed and selected my best gown. It was a green muslin, high waisted and loosely flowing, and still very fashionable. Effie ignored fashion, and still wore the style of her youth, with a hoop underneath her skirt. No amount of entreaties on my part would make her change her mind. I completed my toilet and hurried downstairs.

Effie was in the kitchen mixing a spice barm cake.

"Sunday-best today," she commented as I walked in. "I've just boiled you an egg, and there's plenty of bread and butter."

"Thank you, Effie. I'm sorry I'm late. I overslept."

"It doesn't matter," she said, washing the cake mixture off her hands in a pail of water kept for the purpose. "It did you good. You're looking a lot better today."

I sat down and buttered a slice of bread.

"I spoke to Father last night about an iron range, and he said you can have one."

She looked at me in amazement as she dried her hand on the kitchen towel.

"I can really have one! Oh, Mary, I can't believe it."

She picked up the tea-pot and topped it up with boiling water from the old black kettle on the fire. As she did so the back door opened, and Christmas Boultbee entered, carrying a dead hen. He was an old man with a shiny bald head, not a tooth in his head, and a grey stubble on his chin. His shirt and breeches were heavily stained—in fact I had never seen him in clean clothes—and there was the usual odour of the cow-byre about his boots.

He grinned at me.

"Hello, Christmas. How's life?"

"Fair to middling," he replied, walking across the room. "They told me you was back. I wouldn't live in Brummagen for all the tea in China. Them dark dirty factories would be the death of me. Rose will be glad to see you."

"How is she?"

"Getting prettier every day."

Then he turned his attention to Effie, who was, after all, the reason for his visit.

"How's Effie, my love, today? Oh, the sight of you fills me with desire! If it weren't for you, I'd leave this place tomorrow."

Effie ignored him and bent down to

sweep the hot wood ash out of the beehive oven. We still retained this antiquated method of baking. Wood had been placed inside the oven and set alight, and the heat from the burning wood was retained by the bricks that lined the oven. When the fire died down, the ashes were swept out and the baking began.

Whilst Effie was still bending down, Christmas took advantage of her vulnerable position and gave her a resounding smack on the buttocks.

Effie put her brush down and spun round, her face flushed and embarrassed.

"How dare you do that, Christmas Boultbee! Whatever will Mr. Dordon think?"

"Mr. Dordon ain't here to see it."

"Well, just you have a bit more respect."

"I've got plenty of respect for you, Effie, my love."

"Well, you don't show it."

"Oh, don't I. Well, look what I've brought for you." And he held up the dead hen. "Here you are. You can have a roasted chicken for your supper tonight."

He handed it to Effie, who held it up in dismay.

"It's only got one leg."

"It got shut in a door."

"Shut in a door? How did that happen?"

"It's a long story. I'll tell you some other time. Ta, ra."

To our relief he opened the back door and was gone. Effie sat down on the stool and gave a big sigh.

"Christmas Boultbee's the plague of my life. I dread him coming in. Roast chicken indeed," she exclaimed, holding up the dead bird. "More likely to be an old boiling fowl. Still it was nice of him to think of me."

She put the bird on a side-table, picked up her brush and shovel, and continued sweeping the ash out of the oven. When she had finished, she put the spice barm cake in the oven and closed the door.

"How are you going to get up to the castle? You've just missed Will Sheepy."

"I'd like to take the pony, but I'd better see first if Father wants her. Do you know where he is?"

"I saw him in the fields by the leat, just before you came down."

I left the house and went round to the back of the mill, past the mill-pond, and along the banks of the leat. This was a canal that had been dug in order to divert the water from the Bourne to the mill-wheel, running in a straight line to the mill-pond, whilst the Bourne continued on its way like a twisted strand of ribbon through our fields.

The land bordering our fields belonged to Diggy Smith. He bred donkeys. Such pretty docile creatures; they would come to the fence and nuzzle one's hand, looking for tit-bits. But today was different. Instead of the donkeys being in Diggy's field, they were in ours, mingling with the cows. There must have been about a dozen of them.

Father was angrily pacing the banks of the leat, his hands behind his back.

"I've got to do something about this,

Mary," he said as I approached. "I'm weary of chasing them back. I believe Diggy deliberately lets them out. Stands to reason. They've eaten his field bare, whereas I've got plenty of grass. There was no trouble from him when he only had a few donkeys, but now, look how many he's got. There must be a dozen there at least. Oh, there's young Nicholas Jeffcoate."

I looked across to the lane to see a young man driving a gig down the hill.

He waved to Nicholas and gestured him to stop. Nicholas waved back.

"Come on," said Father, setting off at a quick pace. "I'd like to have a word with him. He's a doctor now, and done very well for himself. Better than Harry. Remember they used to go to school together?"

We met at the garden gate.

I had not seen Nicholas for years, and as he climbed down from his gig I saw he had grown into a tall, long-legged, solemn young man. He was very smartly dressed for a country doctor in a black top hat, dark coat with gold buttons, and pale grey trousers.

"How are you, Mr. Dordon?" he asked. His voice was quiet and professional. A far cry from the boy I used to know.

"Oh, I'm fine, Nicholas. All due to good doctoring eh? You remember Mary?"

Nicholas bowed politely over my hand.

"Of course I remember you, Mary, but how you have changed."

"For the better I hope," I laughed. "You remember the little girl who couldn't keep her gown clean, who wanted to do all the things boys did, and not sit at home playing with dolls."

He smiled, remembering.

"Come into the house," said Father. "I would appreciate your advice, Nicholas, although it's a matter that's not really your line of country."

Father led the way into the parlour.

"Like a brandy, Nicholas?"

"Not for me, thank you, Mr. Dordon," he replied.

We all sat down at the dining-table.

"What's the trouble, Mr. Dordon?"

"I'm worried about these donkeys. Did you see them as you passed?"

Nicholas nodded.

"As you know they belong to Diggy Smith. The trouble started last summer. Occasionally I would find them in my fields. Now it's several times a week. Diggy says they get out by accident, but I don't believe him. I say he deliberately knocks down a bit of fencing so they can get out and eat my grass. You see, he's increased the numbers and he just hasn't got the grazing for them."

"Charge him for grazing."

"I've tried that. But he says why should he pay because the donkeys accidentally get into my fields."

"I'm afraid he's got to."

"I've told him until I'm blue in the face. He's an obstinate, stupid feller."

"Would you like me to speak to him?"

"I'd be much obliged, Nicholas. I think a third party in this matter would be a great help. Try to make him see sense. I don't want the unpleasantness of taking him to court. I actually like Diggy."

Nicholas rose to go.

"Thanks, Nicholas."

"I understand purple admirals are in this district," he announced as he put on his top hat.

"Purple admirals?" I exclaimed, wondering what he meant.

"Tut, tut, Mary. They're butterflies," he said, gently admonishing me. "Fancy not remembering that. Harry would have remembered. I'm looking for one to add to my collection. Unfortunately the season's finished, and I'll have to wait until next summer now. For sheer grace and beauty there is nothing to equal a purple admiral on the wing. Have you ever watched one emerge from the chrysalis?"

I shamefully shook my head.

"It's one of the miracles of nature," he continued. "You should see my collection some time. I have a Queen of Spain. Very rare in this part of the country. Ever seen one?"

"I'm afraid not."

"You've missed a lot. An astonishing insect. Colouring under the wing looks like solid silver. Well, I'll have to go. I could talk all day about my collection. I'll do my best with Diggy Smith, Mr. Dordon. I think I'll see if he's up there now."

We said good-bye to Nicholas and watched him drive away.

"Very strange," said Father as he closed the door.

"What do you mean?"

"Collecting butterflies of course. He seemed normal enough when he was young."

"It's a harmless interest. May I take the pony to Golding Castle?"

"Certainly," he replied. "And tell Grace it's about time she paid us a visit."

In the kitchen Effie gave me a small basket covered with a linen cloth.

"For your Aunt Grace," she called, as I hurried out to the stables.

I saddled up the pony and set off, splashing through the Bourne, and up the hill. Over to the right I could see Nicholas talking to Diggy Smith. When I reached the top of the hill I could not resist peeping into the basket.

They were Bosworth Jumbles—biscuits made in interlaced rings covered in sugar. How thoughtful of Effie to remember Aunt Grace was fond of them. Effie said Richard III's cook had dropped the recipe on the battlefield at Bosworth in 1485. This I found hard to believe, but I liked the biscuits.

When I reached the turnpike Mr. Dagley let me pass free. This was not surprising considering the money he owed Father.

He closed the gate.

"Will you be at home for a while now?" he enquired idly.

"Yes, I think so. How's Mrs. Dagley?"

"Oh, spending all my money as usual. She says shrouds ain't got pockets. I keep telling her about a rainy day."

Poor man, with a spendthrift wife he was fighting a losing battle. I kept on the turnpike for about half a mile, then turned off onto a quiet lane which skirted the western edge of Golding Wood. After a while a high wall of red sandstone appeared on the right side of the lane, then the wrought-iron gates of Golding Castle, bearing the Drew coat-of-arms, three wrens on a silver shield.

Young Ned Cunningham opened the gates. He had no need to enquire my business—I had been coming to see Aunt Grace since I was a small child.

Beyond the gates lay a straight avenue lined with beeches, at the end of which, framed between the trees, lay the castle gate-house, built of red sandstone with twin towers, and narrow arched windows, and on the righthand tower was a clock, stopped permanently at half-past noon. I always felt time stood still anyway at Golding Castle, and this only served to confirm it.

As I reached the end of the avenue the whole castle came into view. It was an idyllic, changeless scene. Surrounded by a moat, the ancient Norman walls stretched out on either side of the gate-house with a turret at each corner. The drawbridge had been dispensed with in the fifteenth century, and since then a stone bridge had spanned the moat. Today the water lay smooth and shining in the autumn sun, and swans glided silently to and fro.

I passed over the bridge, through the gate-house, and the pony's hooves clattered on the cobblestones in the courtyard.

Here were the castle buildings. On the south side lay the mediaeval part of red sandstone, with a large oak iron-studded door, and arched early English windows. This building housed the great hall.

Adjoining on the eastern side was the Elizabethan timber-framed building with large latticed windows set in square bays. Here were the main living-quarters of the Drew family.

On the west and north sides of the courtyard lay the ruined remains of the mediaeval castle—sections of spiralling stone staircases, crumbling walls, and small mediaeval doors leading to dark, cobwebby store-rooms.

A white peacock, its lacy fan spread, honked at me as it strutted across the cobblestones. I dismounted, and as I knocked at a small door in the mediaeval building I thought I heard the sound of children's voices coming from the castle ruins.

The door was opened by a pretty young girl in a white cap and apron over a mauve gown, the uniform of the castle maids.

"Hello, Lotty. I've come to see my aunt."

"Mrs. Allen," she turned and yelled. "Mary's here."

"All right, Lotty," said a familiar voice. "Keep your voice down. You'll have her ladyship complaining. Come in, Mary."

I walked into the low-ceilinged room with its stone floor, its cast-iron ranges so envied by Effie, its rows of bells along the wall.

Lotty resumed her seat at the kitchen

table with another maid, and they resumed their task of shelling peas, whilst Aunt Grace gave me a hug and a kiss on the cheek.

She was my father's sister, a sturdily built woman in her middle years. A plain, but pleasant face, her fair hair beneath her cap turning grey, her apron spotless and starched as usual, and the keys, the badge of her office, hanging at her waist. She had been housekeeper at Golding Castle as long as I could remember. I liked Aunt Grace. I had never met Mr. Allen. It was a subject shrouded in mystery, and neither she nor Father would ever discuss it.

"What a lovely surprise!" she exclaimed. "But what are you doing here? I thought you were in Birmingham."

Just then a bell on the wall jangled, and Lotty rose wearily to her feet.

"That'll be Miss Emma. Now don't go looking like that. Straighten your cap and tidy up your hair."

Lotty sulkily walked across to a tiny mirror on the wall, hastily straightened her cap, pushed odd wisps of hair beneath it, and hurried from the room.

"You've got to watch these girls all the time, Mary," she whispered to me. "Come into my sitting-room. We can talk there."

She led me down the corridor and opened the door of a comfortable, sunny room. It held an amazing number of plants in little clay pots, that had all been grown from cuttings she had persuaded the castle gardener to give her through the years.

"Are you admiring my plants?" she laughed. "Mr. Boun, the new butler, he says I should have been a gardener. Sit yourself down, Mary, and I'll make you a cup of tea.

"Isn't it lovely now the war's over, and we can have all the tea we want. It used to get such a dreadful taste boiling the same leaves over and over again."

She put the kettle on the fire and spooned tea into a pot.

"Well, and how's my brother?"

"Father's very well, thank you. Having

a bit of trouble at the moment with Diggy Smith and his donkeys."

"Everyone has trouble with the donkey man sooner or later."

I put the basket on the table.

"A present from Effie."

She drew back the linen cloth and smiled.

"Bosworth jumbles!" she exclaimed. "Do thank her for me. I'll say this for Effie. She couldn't say boo to a goose, but she's a good biscuit maker and her pork pies are a treat."

She offered me one, and took one herself.

"Hmm! Delicious! I don't know how she puts up with my brother George. George is all right, but like all the menfolk, he does like to have his own way. She ought to stand up for herself more."

"Father's going to buy her one of those cast-iron ranges."

"About time too. George has been doing very nicely these last few years. As the price of grain went up, so did his charges. Now you didn't come here to talk about Effie and your father. Why aren't you in Birmingham?"

She handed me a cup of tea.

"I couldn't work there any longer, Aunt Grace."

She gave me a quick, knowing look.

"Like that, was it. I have maids leaving here all the time." She lowered her voice. "Sir Francis—lecherous old . . . he can't keep his hands off them. If they're young and pretty, it's just a question of time. Of course Lady Eleanor turns a blind eye. Pretends she doesn't know. I feel sorry for her. Well, what are you going to do now? Marry Mr. Hastilow?"

She gave me a wink.

"You know I don't want to do that."

"I was only joking. Anyway, I hear he's away at present." She sipped her tea in silence for a few minutes. Then she put the cup down. "You play the pianoforte, Mary. Didn't you teach it in Birmingham?"

"Yes—why do you ask?"

"It's Lady Eleanor. She's looking for

someone to teach the pianoforte to Miss Caroline and Master Jamie. They've come to live here—they're Master Robert's children. Of course she would want to know the reason why you left your last post."

I pondered a moment on this.

"The family were discussing going to India, and of course I would not have gone with them."

Aunt Grace looked at me thoughtfully.

"You see, a governess has already started, but she doesn't teach music, and Lady Eleanor's very keen on it. Would you like me to have a word with her ladyship about you?"

"Er . . . yes."

"Wait here a moment."

She was back in ten minutes, and looking very pleased with herself.

"Lady Eleanor will see you right away. Don't look so worried, Mary. She's very nice, and she remembers you."

We crossed the courtyard and entered the Elizabethan house. Then along a corridor when carpet underfoot silenced our feet, and on the walls were closely hung portraits of past members of the Drew family. Finally she paused before a cream-painted door and opened it. We walked into a charming little sitting-room that looked onto the courtyard. Scattered around the room were elegant armchairs in the French style, and arranged before the window was an ottoman couch covered in striped silk.

"Now, you'll be all right, Mary. She won't be a moment."

Giving me a reassuring smile, she closed the door, and I was alone.

I felt quite ill-at-ease as I paced the floor. It had all happened so suddenly. Was I good enough to teach the piano-forte to the granddaughter of a baronet? Such people usually employed Italian music masters. I took a deep breath. It was too late to change my mind. I was here, and I would have to go through with it.

I was admiring a painting over the fireplace of knights jousting at Smithfield when the door behind me opened. I turned expecting to see Lady Eleanor.

I thought my heart was going to stop beating.

Charles Field was standing in the open doorway.

4

THE shock of seeing him again was so overwhelming I found my legs were trembling. I hastily sat down on the nearest chair.

"Mary, what are you doing here?"

His tone was one of pleasurable surprise, almost as if nothing had happened. I controlled my anger, there was nothing to be gained, and answered in a cold voice.

"There is a possibility of teaching the pianoforte to Lady Eleanor's grand-daughter."

Last week I had thought he was a friend; now he was an opponent I must fight. I got up and walked to the window wishing with all my heart I had never agreed to see Lady Eleanor. A fat, black fly buzzed against the pane.

"Teaching the pianoforte?" he exclaimed in surprise. "And what about

Cathy and Jane? You were teaching them. My stepmother could not make head nor tail of your letter. Neither could I. Why did you run away?"

"Don't you think that an extraordinary question to ask," I said, making an effort to keep calm.

"Mary, I must speak to you privately, not here. Actually the only reason I am at Golding Castle is to see you."

"To see me?" I exclaimed in disbelief, still gazing through the window.

"Yes. Robert and I are in the same regiment. He invited me for a bit of shooting. It was a loose arrangement and I had decided not to come, but when I learnt you lived only a few miles away . . ."

"You decided to continue the pursuit."

"I wouldn't put it that way." He paused.

"What's the matter, Mary? You've changed. Why don't you look at me?"

He walked across and stood behind me, placing his hand lightly on my arm. I felt myself stiffen at his touch.

"I went for a ride with Robert this morning." His voice was low and gentle. "And I saw your father's mill in the valley. I'll come there tonight."

I turned quickly and faced him.

"No. That's not possible."

"We'll meet somewhere else then," he said lightly. "This morning I noticed there was a stile half-way down the slope between the wood and your father's mill," he continued. "I'll meet you there. It will be late I'm afraid. About ten. The Drews dine rather late. Find some excuse to get away."

My agony was cut short by the door opening, and Lady Eleanor entered. A short lady, rather stout, with sagging cheeks and a sagging bosom. She moved forward with a rustle of silk, her face unsmiling. Her husband's blatant infidelities made her a lonely figure, and she wore her loneliness like a veil.

"Good morning, Lady Eleanor."

Charles clicked his heels and gave a short bow.

"Good morning, Charles. Just off shooting?"

"Yes, but we're having a bit of trouble getting enough beaters."

"Take the gardening boys. You mustn't let your shooting be spoilt for want of beaters."

"Thank you. If you'll excuse me, I'll tell Robert."

The door closed and I was alone with Lady Eleanor.

"Miss Dordon. Please sit down."

She motioned me to sit in one of the armchairs whilst she seated herself on the couch. Through the window Charles crossed the courtyard. Last week seemed a lifetime away. I had a dreadful desire to weep. Lady Eleanor followed my glance.

"Such a pleasant man," she observed. "He and my daughter Emma are very good friends. Now Miss Dordon. I remember you very well. Your father's the miller and you've been visiting your aunt, Mrs. Allen, since you were a little girl. Isn't that so?"

I nodded, giving a nervous smile.

"I pride myself on knowing most people round here," she continued, arranging the folds of her gown. "Now Mrs. Allen tells me you teach the pianoforte. I am in such a quandary at the moment. You probably heard that Robert's wife died earlier this year, such a sad time. And the children, Caroline and Jamie, have been living in London with Robert's mother-in-law. A good woman and I do admire her, but I'm afraid the children proved a little too much for her, so Robert arranged for them to come here about a month ago.

"We have engaged a governess, Miss Plum, an excellent woman, but unfortunately she does not teach music. Jamie will be going to Eton in a few years, but it's mainly Caroline that concerns me. A woman's place is to charm and amuse, don't you think, and for this reason I want her to learn to play the pianoforte.

"You wouldn't believe the difficulty I have had in trying to find a suitable person. Now I understand you were trained at Miss Digbeth's Academy, and were recently teaching in Birmingham. I won't bother about references because I have known your family all my life."

I breathed a sigh of relief.

"Would you like to take the post?"

"I would be pleased to, Ma'am."

"Good. I always feel confident employing local people. Well, that's settled. Three mornings a week. And would half a guinea a week be satisfactory?"

It was more than satisfactory.

"You are very generous. Would you like your grandson to have lessons?"

"I doubt if Jamie will be interested. He's such a mischievous little boy. Completely undisciplined."

She pulled the silken bell-rope to denote the interview was finished.

"I'll let you know when it will be convenient to start."

"Thank you, Ma'am."

The door opened and a footman appeared.

"Miss Dordon is leaving."

Giving Lady Eleanor a short curtsey, I followed the footman from the room.

I knew most of the servants in the castle, and this young man was Hopper's brother.

"Mrs. Allen wants to see you before you go," he whispered as we walked along the corridor. "How did you get on with the old dragon?"

"She's not so bad," I said.

Half a guinea for three mornings' work! It was incredible, and more than that, I loved to play the pianoforte, and sadly missed there not being one at the mill. Now I would be able to play it every week.

He left me at the door of Aunt Grace's sitting-room. I gave a little tap on the door.

"Come in," called Aunt Grace.

I opened the door to find her adding up her accounts book. She closed the book and beamed at me.

"Well, how did you get on with her ladyship?"

"Very well. She's engaged me."

"I'm so pleased, Mary. It will be lovely having you working here. I once heard you play at your Aunt Esther's. Oh, here's Effie's basket."

She walked with me through to the kitchen where the maids were now peeling potatoes.

"We're in such a rush at the moment, and short-handed. A friend of Master Robert's arrived yesterday. Such a nice man. We're going to have a special dinner tonight. Well, any visitor who fought Boney deserves special attention." She moved towards the door. "I've been hearing rumours that Miss Emma's going to get wed."

"Where's Alice?" I asked, suddenly realising she was missing. It was also a good opportunity to change the subject.

Her face stiffened, and the maids stopped working and stared at me.

"You mean Alice Tull?"

"Yes."

"Don't you know?"

"Know what?"

She opened the door and we stepped out into the courtyard.

"I don't like discussing it in front of the maids. It upsets them so. She was found murdered in Golding Wood."

"Murdered? When did this happen?"

"Oh, a long time back. Must have been in the summer. But what was so awful she didn't have any clothes on, and she was holding a bunch of flowers. It was horrible."

"Poor Alice. Did they find out who had done it?"

"No. The constable came up asking questions, but he couldn't find out anything. She had been meeting someone on her days off, I know that, but she never discussed who it was. Alice used to keep her business private." She lowered her voice to a whisper. "I know Sir Francis fancied Alice. It makes you think, doesn't it."

I mounted the pony.

"Don't take the short cut through the wood," she warned. "Lady Eleanor won't allow any of the maids in there now."

"I won't Aunt Grace. Good-bye, and thanks for speaking to Lady Eleanor for me."

"I'd do anything for you, Mary. Give my best wishes to your father and thank Effie for the jumbles. Good-bye, Mary. Take care."

I went out through the gate-house and over the bridge. Now I knew the meaning of Effie's look.

Taking Aunt Grace's advice I turned the pony's head in the direction of Golding Magna. In the distance was the sound of sporadic shooting. My thoughts turned to Charles. He had lied to me. The real purpose of his visit was to see Emma Drew.

I entered Golding Magna, a pretty village of timber-framed cottages with thatched roofs clustered around the Wheatsheaf. Today the place was deserted except for a solitary dog asleep in the middle of the road. I rode round him and took the lane to Golding Parva.

It was such a beautiful day I could not remain angry towards anyone for long, and soon my thoughts towards Charles softened. He had said he wanted to see me tonight. Perhaps I should go and hear what he had to say?

At Golding Parva I turned left. After about half a mile the lane started to descend, and our valley from the southern end unfolded before me with Golding Wood looking like an olive-green smudge on a painter's canvas. And I remembered poor Alice Tull, and I remembered her hair. Thick, black tresses that fell to her waist. Strange I would never see her again.

Another half-mile and the mill came into view. The doves were sitting on the apex of the stable roof, white and pure, symbols of peace. Hopper was helping Danny unload sacks of grain from a cart outside, and as I stabled the pony, Hopper left his unloading and walked across to me. His face looked pale and strained as he leaned over the stable-door.

"What's the matter, Hopper? Do you feel ill?"

"I'm not ill," he replied. He forced a smile.

"There is something wrong," I insisted.

"Why should there be?" he replied defensively. I came out of the stable and closed the door.

"I'm sorry, Hopper. My mistake."

I started to walk away. He followed.

"Mary."

I stopped.

"Yes, Hopper."

"There is something wrong."

"Rose?"

He nodded.

"She won't go with me to the barn dance tonight. What's wrong with me?"

There was such a note of despair in the young man's voice it touched my heart. "She used to go with me," he continued sadly. "I've always known Rose wasn't in love with me, but I never gave up hope. Now I feel something's happened. She's changed."

Get another girl, Hopper, I thought, but I said what he wanted me to say:

"You may still win her yet. Never give up. You're as good as the next man."

"Thanks, Mary, you've cheered me up."

But I knew he did not mean it. I watched him walk back to the cart. Hopper had changed too. I had never seen him depressed before.

Deciding to have a tactful word with Rose, I walked round to the back of the mill. The dairy door was open, and I walked into the empty room. Rose must have gone to the cow-byre for milk. It was always cold in here, having only a small northern window, and always clean, the tiled floor being washed every morning.

Round the room ran the thrawl. This was bricked, arched recesses where milk in copper cans was stored, and cream in earthenware bowls covered in muslin cloths. On top of the thrawl lay Rose's freshly churned butter in wooden dishes. In the centre of the room was the butter-churn and cheesepress. The sound of approaching footsteps made me turn, and Rose entered carrying a pail of milk.

"Mary!" she exclaimed, putting the pail down and flinging her arms around me. "What a lovely surprise!"

Christmas was right. Rose was getting prettier every day. Her face was like a flower, and her hair was so fair, it was almost the colour of silver, although today I could see very little of it, most of it being tucked beneath her frilly mob-cap.

Hopper had been in love with Rose ever since the first day he had come to work for us. It was not surprising, and there were other young men, too, eager to be her sweetheart.

But unfortunately Rose was ambitious. She had once confided in me that she wanted to marry a gentleman, but in the course of her social round, which was confined to barn dances and village feasts, she never met one. For Rose considered a man could not be a gentleman unless he had money.

"It's so good to see you again," she said enthusiastically.

She poured the milk into the butter-churn.

"There's a barn dance tonight at Charity Farm." There was an excited note in her voice. "Will you be coming?"

I hesitated. I still had not made up my mind about Charles' request to meet tonight.

"Everyone's going," she added encouragingly.

"I'll go another time, Rose."

"What's the matter? You always enjoy a barn dance." Then she looked at me thoughtfully. "Why have you come home so suddenly? Effie said you liked it there."

"I'd rather talk about it another time, Rose."

She put the empty pail on top of the thrawl.

"You'll feel better if you tell me about it," she said sympathetically.

I hesitated. How could I tell her what had happened at the Field house two nights ago? I could not tell anyone.

"If you won't tell me, I'll have to guess,

Mary." Then she paused and gave me a knowing smile. "Last time you were home you told me Mr. Field had a son by his first wife. He was in the army in the Low Countries. He has come on leave and fallen in love with you. Am I right?"

"He's not in love with me," I replied hotly.

"There!" laughed Rose. "I knew I'd get at the truth." She put her arm around me. "Of course he is, Mary. And I can't imagine why you came home."

"Rose. He isn't for me. Men like Charles Field do not marry a miller's daughter. I don't belong to his class."

"Class! It doesn't come into it. If a man loves a woman he doesn't care what her background is."

"Rose, that isn't true, not in real life."

This conversation was not helping Hopper. I decided to steer it towards the barn dance as best I could.

"What will you wear tonight?"

"I have a beautiful new gown. Aunt Nancy gave it to me last night. You should see it—a ribbed pink silk."

It was new for Rose, for her aunt worked as a nursery maid in a lawyer's house at Coleshill. Her employer gave her cast-off clothing, and she in turn passed items onto Rose.

"You'll be the best-dressed girl at the dance. Hopper will be falling more in love with you than ever."

"I'm not going with Hopper. It isn't fair to keep accepting his invitations and giving him false hope. I could never love him, Mary. One day he'll find the right girl."

"Who are you going with?"

She smiled shyly.

"I can't say. Not just at the moment. But I promise you I will, later on. You know we've always shared secrets."

"Of course we have."

"What are you going to do, now that you're at home?"

"I've just come from Golding Castle. I'm going to teach music there."

"Congratulations. I suppose you heard all about Alice while you were up there?"

"I did. It was a terrible shock, and I hear the murderer's never been found."

Rose gave a shiver.

"He's probably still in the district. Oh, I don't want to talk about it. Well, I'd better be getting on with the butter-making, otherwise I won't be going to the dance at all."

I left Rose busily churning, and went down the passage to the kitchen. Effie sat before the fire plucking the hen Christmas had given her.

"Well, how did you get on?" she enquired eagerly as I entered.

I put Effie's basket on the table.

"I had a long interview with Lady Eleanor, and she wants me to teach the pianoforte to Caroline—that's her grand-daughter. They'll let me know when I start. I owe it all to Aunt Grace. Oh, she thanks you for the biscuits."

"Grace is a good woman." She paused in her plucking and smiled. "I'm so pleased. It's just what you wanted. Home every night instead of living in some stranger's house. Home is the best place for you, Mary."

"Effie, why didn't you tell me about Alice Tull?"

"Your father doesn't like me talking about it," she said with a pained expression on her face. "It upsets him. She used to call here with her father when she was little to pick up flour. All we can do is pray for her. I suppose Grace told you."

"Yes."

Effie finished the plucking and put the bird on the table.

"It won't be much of a supper tonight."

"Could I do anything to help?"

"Pick me some sage, will you, Mary?"

I walked out into the garden, and down the path to the corner where the sage grew amongst the camomile, the gold of pleasure, and the horse-tails.

"Mary!"

Hugh Morganwy's voice made me turn. He was walking towards me down the path, and looking very pleased with himself.

"Mary, I've been trying to find you all morning."

"Oh, I'm sorry, Hugh. I've been at Golding Castle."

"You do mix in high society."

"Not really. I was looking for a position."

"A beautiful girl like you should have no need to work."

"You're a flatterer!"

He gave me a disarming smile. "It does no harm." Then he paused and looked almost embarrassed. "It's my birthday today."

"Happy birthday, Hugh."

"Thank you, Mary. I've decided to have a little party tonight. It will be a very simple affair, and I would like you, and Mr. Dordon, and Effie, to come. Hopper says he can't come—has to go to some barn dance. Mr. Dordon has accepted, and I have yet to ask Effie. Will you come, Mary?"

At that moment an open carriage

carrying two women, with a footman standing at the rear, drove past the mill. One of the women was Lady Eleanor, and the other her daughter Emma—a lovely young woman dressed completely in white and holding a white frilly parasol over her dainty pretty head.

"They'll be taking the lunch to the shooting-party," observed Hugh as we watched the carriage ford the Bourne and start to climb the hill.

I had a quick vision of Charles lunching with Emma Drew.

"I shall be pleased to accept your invitation, Hugh."

5

WE set off at sunset in the mill-cart. Father had changed into his Sunday-best specially for the occasion. I thought he looked very smart in his dark tail-coat, and a new black hat with a broad brim turned up at the sides. Effie sat between us in her best linsey-woolsey gown beneath her cloak, and her old straw bonnet tied under the chin with a faded blue ribbon.

"Fancy Hugh inviting me," she kept saying, as she excitedly clutched the spice barm cake on her lap. "And wasn't it lucky I decided to make a cake today, otherwise I wouldn't have had anything to give him."

We followed the turnpike as far as Nether Asterley, a busy village where horses were changed and travellers took refreshments. Then taking the first turning after the village we found ourselves in a narrow lane with Hugh's cottage on the right.

It was now twilight and difficult to see very much of it except that it was built at the edge of the lane and was very small. Hugh was perched up a ladder repairing the roof working by the light of a lantern.

As we approached he gave a shout and came down the ladder.

"I want to get the roof repaired before the winter weather sets in," he said as Father tethered the horse to an old tree-stump. "Welcome to my ruin."

"I'm sure it's not as bad as that," said Effie.

"Wait until you've seen the inside."

He pressed the latch of the cottage door, and led us into a short stone passage, the paint flaking off the walls, an unmistakable smell of dampness in the air.

He insisted on showing us round to prove his point, even though we were ready to believe him. By the light of his lantern he showed us broken windows, plaster bursting off walls, doors hanging on one hinge, and upstairs the hole in the roof where the rain poured in.

"When you offered me a job last summer I had to find somewhere to live quickly. This was all I could find. But I shall gradually get the place repaired, and when I've finished it will be one of the best cottages in Nether Asterley."

We returned to the ground floor, and Hugh showed us into a comparatively pleasant room. There was a cheerful log fire burning in the hearth. Several wooden stools were scattered about the room, a table, and to my astonishment, a harp. It was very old, and battered-looking.

"That harp belonged to my grandfather," he said proudly in answer to my surprised look. "I had quite a job getting it here, I can tell you. Now take off your cloaks, and make yourselves at home."

We took off our cloaks, and Effie shyly gave him the cake with our best wishes, whilst Father produced a bottle of wine.

"You didn't give me time to buy you a gift," I said, feeling a little embarrassed.

"You have come and that is enough."

He gave me such a good-natured smile I felt I was foolish to worry about it.

"Nowt like a good fire," exclaimed Father, warming his hands before the blaze. "Evenings are getting chilly now. Mind you, we've had a good autumn—sunniest, driest autumn I can remember. Of course, I don't want it too dry—"

"Or too wet," smiled Hugh. "It is a difficult life being a miller."

Hugh poured out the wine into four old pewter goblets. We appeared to be the only guests.

"Happy birthday, Hugh," said Father, raising his goblet.

"Happy birthday," we echoed.

Effie cut and handed round the cake.

"You shouldn't be living on your own," said Father.

"I agree with you," answered Hugh. Was there the suggestion of a wink in his eye when he looked at me? I wasn't sure.

"Very good of you to invite us," continued Father. "I don't get out much, and have the chance of hearing a bit of music. Except Sundays, and that's church music. I take it you will be playing that there harp."

"I most certainly will," answered Hugh, refilling the goblets.

"One day I shall buy Mary a pianoforte then she can play to me in the evenings. But there's always something. Six years ago it was the Bourne flooding the mill. The damage it did, and the money I had to pay out. Well, let's have a bit of a tune. Do you know 'The Widow of Huntingdon'?"

Hugh sat down at the harp. He either ignored him or did not hear him. He placed his fingers on the strings, and for the first time I noticed what elegant hands he had for a man, what long sensitive fingers. Then the sound that came from that harp was quite extraordinary. It was as delicate as the clouds moving across the heavens, as gentle as a breeze stirring the grass. Then the sound changed and it became a waterfall roaring down a mountain-side.

I sat entranced. I have never heard such playing, not even at the Birmingham

Town Hall. Then he sang a Welsh ballad in such a beautiful tenor voice it did not seem to matter we could not understand the words.

"That was the story of Twm Sion Cati," he said when the song came to an end.

"Who was he?" asked Father, looking very puzzled.

"He was the Welsh Robin Hood."

"I never knew there was a Welsh Robin Hood," said Effie in a forlorn voice.

Hugh refilled our goblets, and then reseated himself at the harp. He struck a chord, and started to sing again, this time in English.

The centuries rolled back, and he sang of Vortigen and Ambrosius and Llywellyn. He sang of battles, of treachery, of love. The song finished and the entrancement ended. There was silence for a moment, no one moved, then we clapped our appreciation.

It was at this point I realised that Effie was weeping. Her head bent down, her breast shaking, as the tears rolled down her soft pink cheeks. But it was not the music that had caused this emotional outburst.

"I shouldn't have had that last goblet. Too much wine always makes me cry." And she burst into fresh sobs.

Father had no patience.

"What did you drink it for then?" he demanded. "Stop crying this instant."

But the flood-gates were open, and Effie could not stop.

"She's ruined the evening," said Father in a furious tone. "She should never have come."

"Don't be too hard on her, Mr. Dordon," said Hugh.

"We'd best get her home," Father replied, putting on his coat. "We can't sit here listening to that. I'm sorry, Hugh. It's been a wonderful evening, listening to you. I didn't know you had such a voice. Mr. Hastilow will be after you to sing in the church choir."

"Well, no thank you, Mr. Dordon. I'm not much of a church-goer."

I put Effie's cloak around her

shoulders, and her bonnet upon her head. As we said our good-byes at the door, Effie gave Hugh an unexpected kiss on the cheek, then walked unsteadily to the cart. I had not realised she was drunk. I helped her up into the seat, and placing her head upon my shoulder, she slept.

"You wouldn't think she was a parson's daughter," fumed Father as we drove off.

I kept a firm arm around Effie. After a while she started to snore.

"You can't take her anywhere," Father shouted as we drove through Nether Asterley. "Give her a drop of liquor, and she'll make a fool of herself."

"She couldn't help it, Father. Anyway, it's partly my fault. I forgot alcohol has this effect on Effie. I should have told Hugh not to give her more than one goblet."

It was a cold night with a mist coming up, and I shivered a little as we trotted along the turnpike, and then turned off into our lane.

"It was a marvellous evening," said Father, starting to relent. "Despite Effie.

What a voice! And the way he plays that harp! It was a lucky day for me when he passed through Golding."

Hugh puzzled me. He was the most unusual mill-hand Father had ever employed.

"Why did Hugh leave Wales?"

"His father died last year," he replied. "Left on his own on this sheep farm up in the Black Mountains, it must have been very lonely for him. You can't blame him for wanting to come to England and see a bit of life. He ought to get himself a wife and settle down."

He was an attractive man too, I thought. Then I wondered how he had managed to remain single for so long.

We were now going down the hill into our little valley. A horse whinnied among the trees. Father put on the brake and we came to a slow stop. There was always the possibility that one of our horses had got out.

Tethered amongst the trees by the lane-side was a horse harnessed to a gig. I had seen that gig somewhere before. It was an expensive-looking vehicle with a lot of brass ornamentation.

Father remembered.

"That's Nicholas' gig," he exclaimed in a bewildered tone. "What on earth is he doing here at this time of night? If someone was ill at Hastilows, he wouldn't leave his gig down here. I wonder what he's up to?"

We continued down the hill.

"There's something definitely queer about a man who collects butterflies," he said thoughtfully. "Anyway, if he convinces Diggy Smith he has to pay grazing rights, I'll reconsider my opinion."

Father was a fair man.

We forded the Bourne and stopped outside the mill. As it proved impossible to awaken Effie, we had no alternative but to carry her into the mill, and up the stairs to her room.

It was a long slow struggle, particularly the stairs, but finally we reached her room and laid her on the bed. Father went downstairs, grumbling, to stable the horse.

I gently removed her bonnet, took off her spectacles and put them on the little table next to the stuffed owl. Then unlaced her boots and pulled them off. It was the least I could do, I reflected, for all the love and understanding she had shown me through the years. Covering her with a thick blanket, I tiptoed from the room and went downstairs.

Father was stirring the dying embers of the fire with the old poker.

"You know, Mary, I think I've been too hard on Effie. We all have our weaknesses. And we must never forget to thank God for all the good things he bestows on us. Good health for instance. How we take that for granted. Sometimes we think we're going to live forever. But we're not. I realised that this summer when I was ill. In fact I made my will. I've left the mill to Harry, and in the event of you not marrying, which is highly unlikely, my girl, the income from the farm would be yours."

"You're not going to die, Father, not for a very long time, because I'll see you take care of yourself."

Father sat down on the settle and lit his pipe.

"Good night, Mary. You're a good girl."

"Good night, Father."

I went up to my room. It had been a lovely evening, although I wish Father had not spoken about dying, I thought as I climbed into bed. The church clock at Golding Parva struck the half-hour. It must be half-past ten, and I suddenly remembered Charles, and his request to meet me at the stile.

He was playing a game with me, I thought bitterly, and as I fell asleep I wondered at his next move.

I awoke the following morning to a sensation of silence. From the window the valley was filled with mist, and all within the mill was stilled.

It must be very early, I thought. Then Father's footsteps hurried past my door. He would be on his way to the mill-pond to open the sluice-gate. The white doves flew past the window to take their morning dip in the Bourne. I got out of bed and watched them preening and shaking their pretty feathers at the water's edge. Then I heard the sudden rush of water, and the wheel started to turn, and from within the mill came the soft muffled sounds of machinery turning.

The mill was like an old man stirring.

Dressing quickly in the chilly atmosphere, I found myself wondering what Nicholas Jeffcoate was doing in our valley last night. What could he have been doing in the dark?

When I walked into the kitchen there was already a good fire blazing in the ingle-nook. Whatever happened, Effie was always up first. She was frying bacon in a large pan over the fire, a tired, worried expression on her face.

"I made a fool of myself last night," she said as I walked in. "I don't know what came over me, drinking all that wine when I know the effect it has on me. I'll never forgive myself for spoiling your evening."

"You didn't spoil the evening. We all enjoyed it. Now don't give it another thought."

"I'll swear this on the Bible. I'll never touch another drop as long as I live."

She put a plate of bacon in front of me.

"What's happening today?"

"Christmas is killing a pig."

And a smile lit up her face. Effie could not remain miserable for long, for this was the time of the year she liked best anyway. After the pig was killed, it was cut up and salted, then pork suppers were held and neighbours invited to partake of dishes of succulent roasted pork and apple sauce. With the return of hospitality these pork supper parties could last until Christmas.

Effie was back to normal now.

"I want to get a lot of bread baked today," she continued, "because tomorrow I'll be salting."

"I'll help you, Effie."

"Thanks, Mary." She picked up the

tea-pot and poured out two cups. "While I was out looking for eggs a short while back I met Christmas. He said Rose didn't come home last night. He's very angry. I hope she hasn't run off with a soldier like that Fanny Draycote from Over Whitacre."

She looked at me for my opinion.

"Rose wouldn't do a silly thing like that," I answered. "She's not that sort. She has a lot of sense. She'd see she had the blessing of the church first."

"Christmas says when she does come home he'll beat the living daylights out of her. There's the barracks at Camp Hill other side of Atherstone. Happen she knew one of the soldiers from there. Young girls do such silly things. All they can see is his handsome looks. They never think of tomorrow."

I drank the tea, pondering about Rose. Strange she would not tell me who had asked her to the dance. It was unlike her, she was always so frank and open. I felt perturbed—a feeling something was wrong. Had she run away with a soldier like Effie suggested? I decided I must speak to Hopper. Ask him a few tactful questions. He would surely put my mind at rest.

Leaving Effie putting eggs in the basket for the eggman, I walked through the parlour to the weighing-room. As I opened the door Hugh and Father were watching the cogs on the drive.

"There's two there need renewing," shouted Father over the noise. "You need apple wood or beech."

"I'll do it for you, Mr. Dordon," Hugh shouted back.

Through the window Danny was loading sacks of flour onto a cart. Hopper was nowhere to be seen.

Hugh looked up and saw me.

"How's Effie this morning?" he smiled.

"Full of contrition. Swears she'll never touch another drop."

Hugh laughed.

"Where's Hopper?" I asked.

"I haven't seen him," Hugh replied.

"He hasn't turned up for work, that's why," retorted Father. "And when he does, I'll have a few words to say to him. I suppose he's sleeping it off somewhere. Why do you want him?"

"Rose didn't go home last night, and I was going to ask him if he knew what had happened to her. Christmas is very worried."

"And I'm worried too about the work that's not being done here. I've got the castle waggon arriving any time. And there'll be no butter and cheese ready for Friday market. I'm going to get some breakfast."

And with that he strode angrily from the room. Hugh gave me a sympathetic smile as he walked away.

I decided to question Danny. Sometimes he went to the Charity Farm barn dances, and I might get some sense out of him. I went outside and found him leaning over the tail-board watching the driver tying up a sack. His head was white with flour. He always managed to get himself in a mess, it seemed inevitable.

"What happened, Danny?"

"One of the sacks come undone," he replied glumly.

"Did you go to the barn dance last night," I enquired as casually as I could.

His face broke into a big grin.

"Yes, Mary. I like the fiddles. I wish I could play a fiddle."

"Did you see Rose there?"

"Yes, Mary, and she looked very pretty."

"Who was she with?"

He looked puzzled and frowned at me.

"The man with Rose. What was his name?"

"Hopper. She always goes with Hopper."

I felt perplexed. Hopper had been upset because she would not go with him. She must have changed her mind at the last minute.

"Hopper was angry with Rose."

"Why was he angry?"

A pained expression came on Danny's face.

"I don't know. Why are you asking all

these questions. I never drank no ale. I never did nothing bad."

"Of course you didn't. It's just that Rose didn't go home last night and we're a little worried. Did Hopper leave the dance with her?"

He shook his head vigorously.

"Rose went home alone. I saw her. I saw her run down the lane. I followed her a bit, but she shouted to me 'go away'."

"Why did you follow her?"

"I don't know," he said lamely. "I think it was because she's pretty."

"What did you do after that?"

"I think I went back to the barn. Mary, these questions are making my head ache."

"I'm sorry, Danny. I've finished now."

I went back into the mill. I was worrying unnecessarily. Rose would be back before the day ended, I thought as I walked along the passage and into the dairy. She would have some reasonable explanation and the whole business would be forgotten. As for Hopper, he had drunk too much and overslept. As simple as that.

I cut a wedge of butter for household use, and just as I was leaving I noticed Rose was in the middle of making slip-coat, a type of cheese that required daily attention otherwise it was ruined. Rose was a conscientious dairymaid. She would be back.

I fed the hens and swept the garden paths, and all the time I could not stop thinking about Rose. Rose lived at Golding Magna. If she had left the dance alone, she would not have taken the short cut through Golding Wood, especially since Alice Tull's murder. I decided she had stayed the night somewhere. She had a relation, a distant cousin, living at Gospel Oak.

The castle waggon did not arrive until midday. Will Sheepy the driver climbed down and knocked at the parlour door.

Father opened the door.

"Come in, Will. I was expecting you."

Will stepped into the parlour.

"I'm sorry I'm late. We're a bit short-handed this morning. Oh, I see you're having a bit of lunch. I don't want to intrude."

"Who said you were intruding? Sit down and have a bite to eat with us."

Will Sheepy took the empty chair next to Father. He was an elderly man with a healthy, weather-beaten complexion, side-whiskers, and smartly dressed in a fawn coat and a black top hat. Sir Francis insisted that all castle servants, particularly those whose business took them outside the castle grounds, were well turned out. It reflected on his position. Will never let Sir Francis down. He had worked for him all his life, and nobody could be more loyal than he. Some sneered he had been bought body and soul, but the truth was he had grown very fond of the old man.

Effie set a plate of steaming broth before him.

"Thanks, Effie. I see I came at the right time. That looks real appetising."

"Help yourself to bread, Mr. Sheepy."

Will cut himself a slice of bread and

dipped it in the broth, then paused and looked at me.

"Oh, Mary, I've a message for you. You're to come back to the castle with me."

His eyes twinkled mischievously.

6

"WHAT you been up to, Mary? Master Robert wants to see you."

There was humour in his voice, but Father did not appear to notice it.

"Mary hasn't been up to anything." he interjected, pouring ale into Will's tankard. "Except being engaged to teach pianoforte to his daughter."

There was pride in his voice as he spoke.

"Don't take notice of me, George. You know me better than that. Just having a bit of fun."

Charles would still be there, waiting to continue the pursuit. I felt like a fly being drawn into a web. I made the decision. I was not going to take up the post.

"What's the matter, Mary?" Father's voice was full of concern. "Your face is as long as a poker."

I was a coward. I could not tell him—at least not for the time being.

"It's nothing, Father," I mumbled.

I went up to my room with a sense of guilt. How deep would be his disappointment when he learned the truth, but in the circumstances I felt I had no alternative.

Changing into my grey linen teaching-gown—it seemed the most suitable garment to wear—I stood before the mirror tying my poke-bonnet, trying to decide what excuse I could give to Robert Drew.

I would tell him I regretted the trouble I had caused, but I could not take up the post. Then he would ask the reason, and I could think of none, except the truth. I was a woman fighting to keep her virtue. Such a remark would amuse his father. He liked them to put up a fight. Made the chase more entertaining.

Then I wondered what Robert was like. I had not seen him since I was a child, and all I could remember was a lanky schoolboy.

I went downstairs to the parlour. Will now sat alone at the table. He stood up as I entered.

"I see Danny's finished the unloading. Well, Mary, if you're ready, we'd best be on our way."

I followed Will out to the waggon with a heavy heart. He helped me up into the passenger's seat, then with a curse to the horses, we set off, splashing through the Bourne.

Approaching the top of the hill the sun started to penetrate the mist, turning it into a dissolving golden vapour, rolling back, retreating across the fields, revealing the motionless cattle standing in the wet grass amongst the vetch and shepherd's purse.

"Turned out nice after all," Will commented with a smile.

On we went, past Mr. Hastilow's farm, past the pond, past the blackthorn and scarlet hips, festooned in cobwebs—delicate, lacey patterns hung with tears.

I could see no shape to my future.

"You'll like it up at the castle," he

continued. "Been there forty year, man and boy. And never had no complaint, neither. You do your work, and they'll see you're all right. Miss Caroline's a nice little lady, from what I hear, but they do say her brother, master Jamie, he's a right handful."

On the turnpike Nicholas Jeffcoate passed us and raised his whip in greeting. He was off somewhere in a great hurry.

"The new doctor from Atherstone," commented Will. "Seen him a lot last summer with his butterfly-net." He laughed. "There was an old lady over No Man's Heath way used to do that. Clean off her head she was."

Will kept up a stream of light-hearted gossip as we drove along. The conversation inevitably turned to Alice Tull.

"It were someone she knew," he pronounced ominously as we turned onto the lane that led to the castle.

"Why do you say that?"

"Stands to reason. Alice were a nervous sort of girl. She would never have gone in that wood on her own. Not her.

Someone she knew enticed her in. Someone who lives round here."

We had now reached the castle gates. One of the grooms opened them, and we drove in, along the avenue of beeches, the leaves today falling like golden flakes about our heads.

Approaching the gate-house, Will turned off for the stables and stopped.

"Her ladyship won't allow waggons in the courtyard."

I climbed down and stood hesitantly, the worse was yet to come.

"Now, Mary, remember confidence is a plant of slow growth."

"Yes, Will, I'll remember. Thank you for the ride."

I walked across the bridge. The swans were still gliding peacefully on the water, and today in the courtyard the white peacock strutted with a peahen at his side.

I knocked at the main door in the mediaeval building. It was opened almost immediately by Hopper's brother.

"Hello, Mary. Come in. Master Robert's left a message for you. Will you wait for him in the library. He's out shooting again with his visitor."

He led me up a flight of steps into the great raftered hall.

"That's all he ever does—shooting," he continued. On the walls were oil-paintings of the Drew family ancestors. The men invariably stern, the women pretty, and carved in stone over the great fireplace were the words: "Silence is a goodly virtue." Some of them had not heeded these words for they had ended up in the tower.

At the end of the hall the young footman led me into the library. It was a pleasant, restful room lined with books from floor to ceiling. There were leather armchairs by the fire with a small table by the side of one of them on which rested an open book.

I walked to the window and looked down onto the courtyard where two children now played. They must be Caroline and Jamie.

"You be all right now, Mary? I don't

expect he'll be long. He's been out since breakfast."

Hopper's brother closed the door.

Why does life have to be so complicated, I thought angrily as I walked to and fro. After a while I grew tired of pacing the room and sat down in the armchair by the fire. My eye strayed to the printed page of the open book. It appeared to be a translation of Julius Caesar's *De Bello Gallico*. It seemed very dull to me.

"Miss Dordon, I'm sorry to have kept you waiting."

Robert Drew walked quickly across the room. He had grown into a tall, fair man with gentle, refined features.

"I had expected to be back earlier than this."

I stood up and gave him a quick curtsey.

"Please sit down."

He went and stood with his back to the fire. He was still wearing shooting-clothes —leather breeches with gaiters to the knee.

"Aren't you the miller's daughter from Golding Mill?"

"I am."

I smiled politely.

"I'd just like to ask a few routine questions. I understand my mother has engaged you to teach Caroline the pianoforte. Jamie is too young, and anyway, I think he would much rather climb trees. Everyone says he's difficult, but he just needs care and affection. You know their mother died early this year."

I murmured my condolences.

"Mr. Drew. There is something I have to tell you . . ."

"Where did you learn to play?" he interrupted.

"Miss Digbeth's Academy."

"And who have you taught so far?"

"The Field girls."

"You mean the Birmingham Fields?"

"Yes."

He looked surprised. I waited for him to mention Charles, but he did not.

"How long were you there?"

"Nearly a year."

"Who's your favourite composer?"

"Mozart. Mr. Drew, unfortunately . . ."

"He's mine too."

He looked pleased.

"I'd like to hear you play," he said enthusiastically. "It's a long time since I've heard Mozart. I'll take you to the music-room. We have quite a good pianoforte."

I knew all about the pianoforte at Golding Castle from Aunt Grace. It was an Italian instrument of the best quality. I have my weaknesses, and one of them is pianofortes. I followed him down the narrow spiralling staircase, one hand feeling the wall. I would tell him after I had played I decided.

The staircase led directly into the music-room. It was the most beautiful room I had ever seen. Overhead hung a chandelier of cut glass. On the polished floor were scattered Persian rugs. Around the walls were elegant tapestry chairs, marquetry inlaid cupboards, and a glass cabinet containing Chelsea pottery. And in the centre of the room positioned beneath the chandelier was the pianoforte, made of polished mahogany inlaid with rosewood, with a small stool upholstered in deep blue velvet.

We walked across to the instrument. Robert Drew opened the lid and motioned me to sit.

I seated myself on the velvet stool, feeling nervous and ill-at-ease.

"I presume you can play from memory."

I nodded.

"Play anything you like," he said, folding his arms and leaning on the pianoforte top.

As soon as I struck the first notes of my favourite Mozart sonata my nervousness fled. The tone was superb, and I was conscious of the honour that had been bestowed on me. As I finished I thought I heard footsteps walking away from the closed door.

"Such purity and grace," murmured Robert Drew. "Thank you, Miss Dordon. It was a pleasure listening to you."

As I stood up and closed the lid, the door burst open and the peace of the room was shattered as Caroline and Jamie ran in.

"Stop!" called their father.

The children stopped in the middle of the room, their hands at their sides.

"How many times have I told you—you must not run into a room."

"I'm sorry, Papa," said Caroline, and both children smiled confidently at their father.

Caroline was a pretty child. I judged her to be about ten years old. She had flaxen curls, light blue eyes, and a dimple in her cheek when she smiled. Jamie was as dark as she was fair. A small boy, about seven years old. His smile was not as generous as his sister's.

"This is Miss Dordon," announced their father. "Your new music teacher."

"Mr. Drew, there is something I have to say—"

"Allow me to finish, Miss Dordon, if you please," he rebuked me gently, and then turning to the children continued: "She is going to teach Caroline to play the pianoforte. Jamie is too young at the moment."

Jamie scowled.

"I don't want to play the pianoforte, Papa. I'd rather go shooting with you."

Then Caroline walked shyly up to me, and took my hand.

"Miss Dordon, will you please teach me to play a tune for Papa, before he goes away?"

There was a look of such earnestness on her little face, my heart softened.

"Please, Miss Dordon." She tightened her grip on my hand.

I knew when I was beaten.

"Yes, Caroline."

"Did you want to say something to me, Miss Dordon?"

"It's of no importance," I replied.

"Well, then, I suggest you start the first lesson now."

Caroline clapped her hands with pleasure.

"Don't get too excited, Caroline," her father warned her. "And follow Miss Dordon's instructions."

"Oh, I will, Papa."

"I suggest the next lesson should be the

day after tomorrow, at 11 o'clock. Will that be convenient for you, Miss Dordon?"

"Certainly, Mr. Drew."

"I'll take my leave of you. Good-bye, Miss Dordon. Good-bye, children." And with a wave of his hand he walked from the room.

With suppressed excitement, Caroline seated herself on the pianoforte stool, and arranged the folds of her gown. Jamie started to undo the bow on her sash.

"Now, Jamie," I said, taking the mischievous hands away, and retying the bow, "stand next to me and watch your sister. One day you may be learning yourself."

He stood obediently at my side.

"Caroline, the first thing you have to learn is the names of the notes. This is middle 'C'." And I placed her small thumb on the key. "Now put your first finger on 'D', and your second finger on 'E', your third finger on 'F', and your little finger on 'G'. Can you remember that?"

"Oh yes, Miss Dordon," Caroline

replied eagerly. "Now let me hear you play the notes."

I became absorbed in the lesson, and found myself enjoying teaching her because she wanted to learn. After a while I realised Jamie was not at my side, and on glancing apprehensively round the room caught a glimpse of him on his hands and knees crawling through the legs of the chairs at the far end of the room.

"What are you doing, Jamie?" I called.

"I'm a tiger in the jungle. Papa told me about them."

He did not appear to be doing any harm, and I resumed the lesson. Caroline was now doing the five-finger exercise with both hands. She seemed to have a natural aptitude, and remembered everything I told her. The lesson ended with me showing her how the notes were written down.

"Your first lesson has now ended, Caroline."

She jumped off the stool and slipped her hand into mine.

"Miss Dordon," she said, looking very

serious. "When can I start learning a tune?"

Jamie had disappeared. Where on earth could he be?

"Perhaps at the next lesson," I said, my mind on Jamie. "Jamie. Where are you hiding? Caroline has finished her lesson, and you are to go back to the schoolroom now."

There was a moment's silence, then he appeared from behind a draught screen, an impish expression on his face.

"I hope you've been a good boy."

It must be trying for him, I thought, not having anything to do.

"Do you think you could ask Miss Plum for a picturebook so that Jamie can look at it next time you have your lesson?"

"I'd rather help Garrett pick apples in the orchard." Jamie spoke in a defiant tone.

I closed the pianoforte lid.

"I hate going back to Miss Plum," said Caroline, pulling a sad face.

"That's because we're going to have arithmetic, and Caroline isn't good at it," said Jamie with a lot of satisfaction as they followed me from the room. "I like it, because I'm good at it. Caroline's a duffer."

"I am not."

"Now, children, run along. Miss Plum will be waiting for you."

I stood at the door and watched them run across the courtyard to the Elizabethan house. They were pleasant children, and Jamie was no problem. I had made the right decision to take the post.

I had a long walk home, so postponing a chat with Aunt Grace until another day, I set off immediately across the courtyard, through the gate-house, and down the drive. I was just starting to enjoy walking in the autumn sunshine, but as I neared the gates my pleasure was swept away at the sight of a figure standing across the lane amongst the trees.

It was Charles. There was no escape.

"I've been waiting for you," he spoke in a pleasant tone as I approached.

"How did you know I was in the castle?"

"Heard you playing. Look, Mary, I find

it so difficult to see you privately I thought I'd take the opportunity of escorting you home. It isn't safe anyway for a young woman to walk alone through this wood."

"It's very kind of you, Charles. But it doesn't worry me in the slightest. I've been walking through Golding Wood all my life."

"All the same, I don't think you should take any chances."

I hesitated. The last thing I wanted was to walk through Golding Wood with Charles Field.

"Why didn't you come last night? I waited."

His voice was soft and patient, like speaking to an erring child.

"I'm sorry, Charles, but our friendship must end."

There was a pause, then his voice exploded in anger.

"Why is it wrong to love you?"

"Love?" Now I felt angry. "How lightly you use that word. I don't believe you know the meaning of it."

"Oh, Mary!" And his voice took on a

weary tone. "There's so little time. Don't waste it. I'm returning to my regiment in a few days."

Then he caught my arm and pulled me to him, and his dark eyes searched mine.

"Don't send me back tormented and miserable. Don't treat me in this way, I beseech you. Have you no compassion?"

He was confusing me, sweeping away all my principles of decent behaviour; trying to twist me to his will. I felt his lips brush gently against my cheek, and I could feel myself swaying, tottering.

I heard the clip-clop of an approaching horse. Charles relaxed his grip on my arm, and we both looked round. What a blessed intervention. Nicholas Jeffcoate was approaching in his gig. He drew level and stopped.

"Hello there," he called cheerfully, raising his hat. "Lovely day."

I made an effort to smile.

The two men eyed each other curiously.

"Oh, this is Captain Field—Dr. Nicholas Jeffcoate."

Each man gave a small nod of acknowledgment.

"I have to make a call at Golding Parva," Nicholas continued. "Could I give you a ride back to the mill, Mary?"

"Yes thank you, Nicholas."

"Don't go, Mary." Charles whispered, but the comparative safety of Nicholas' gig was more attractive than Charles' company in Golding Wood.

Without a backward glance I walked across the lane and climbed up next to Nicholas.

We set off down the lane. There was a tight sensation in my chest. I had done what society demanded of me—I had rebuffed the attentions of an amorous gentleman. I should be pleased, but I was not. I felt cold and empty inside.

"I hope I wasn't intruding . . ."

"You weren't, Nicholas," I replied. I could feel my cheeks burning.

"Isn't Captain Field a friend of Robert Drew?"

"They are in the same regiment."

"I thought they must be," he continued. "Not much goes unnoticed in these parts."

He gave me a thoughtful look.

"What are you trying to say?"

"Nothing, Mary, except I hope you know what you're doing."

"I do, Nicholas, and if you don't mind, I don't wish to discuss the matter."

My voice sounded hoarse.

"Of course," he replied quickly.

We drove on for a while, neither of us speaking. I was fighting a strong desire to weep. Then Nicholas broke the silence with a change of subject.

"I have some good news for your father. I'll call in one evening just as soon as I can manage it and tell him the details. Diggy Smith has agreed to pay grazing rights."

He talked continuously after that about the problems that ensue when animals stray onto a neighbour's land. I think it was more out of embarrassment than an interest in the subject.

We reached the mill and I jumped down.

"I hope I haven't offended you, Mary."

"Of course you haven't," I said, trying to smile.

"I say, why don't you come to Atherstone on Saturday and see my Queen of Spain."

His solemn face broke into a slow smile.

I hesitated.

"Bring Effie along as a chaperon, if you wish."

"I'll think about it, Nicholas. You're very kind. Thanks for the ride."

"It's been my pleasure," he called. "Don't forget." And he drove off.

I went first to the byre to see if Christmas had any news of Rose.

The hens followed me into the dimly lit interior. The half-dozen cows we possessed were already in their stalls, filling the atmosphere with that warm animal smell. An occasional tail flicked, a head turned and a soft brown eye stared at me. Over the stalls a rickety ladder led up to the loft, now filled with the new season's hay.

Christmas had started the evening milking, his bald head pressed close against the cow's flanks. His bloodshot eyes looked up at me as I approached.

"Rose were a better milker than me." He said in a rasping voice.

I noticed he spoke in the past tense.

"Any news?" I asked, even though I knew the answer.

He shook his head gloomily, his anger spent.

"She ain't been to her cousin's at Gospel, and her aunt at Coleshill ain't seen her since Monday. I asked a waggoner to call in, and he's just told me. Constable Trye don't like it, and he's getting volunteers together. They're going out tomorrow looking for her."

Then he continued milking.

7

THAT evening during supper we discussed the matter of Constable Trye asking for volunteers to search for Rose.

"I've decided to join them," I told Father and Effie. "I do feel concerned about Rose."

"I'll go too," Effie added. "That is if Mr. Dordon is in agreement."

Father reluctantly gave his consent.

"Hugh and Danny want to go as well. I've told them they can, but I don't like it. Work coming to a stop because Rose is acting the fool." He helped himself to more of Effie's lemon pudding. "Volunteers to go out looking for her—I never heard such nonsense. By the time you get back she'll be here in dairy wondering what possessed you."

"Father, can you suggest what has happened to her?"

"Enjoying herself somewhere, that's what."

The following morning was dull and chilly, with a heavily overcast sky. Constable Trye had asked for everyone to meet at Charity Farm at noon, so Effie and I spent the morning in the dairy salting the pig.

It was a bacon pig that Christmas had killed, and he had left the bacon sides and hams on top of the thrawl. We put on large aprons of sacking to protect our gowns and set to work.

Effie mixed the salt, sugar and saltpetre in a wooden bowl, silently, her lips tight. It was normal for her to sing as she worked, but not today. A heavy oppressive atmosphere hung about the room. We rubbed the mixture into the joints, covering every inch of the surface, no crevice left untouched. It was slow work—a hurried job and the meat would not keep.

It was strange Rose not being there. I missed her carefree chatter, her warm presence.

"She's run away with a soldier," Effie pronounced, scooping up a handful of the salt mixture and rubbing it into a ham joint. "I don't know what Constable Trye is thinking about asking people to go out looking for her."

"You don't have to go, Effie," I said, starting on a bacon side.

"I said I'd go, and I'm not changing my mind."

She hung up the joint on a hook overhead.

"You can't trust men," she sighed. "Look at poor Fanny Draycote. Someone saw her at Market Bosworth, and she's still not wed."

She came across and helped me salt the bacon side, working with her small quick movements. A week from now the process would be repeated, then a month from now the joints would hang in the kitchen to dry.

It was getting late when we had finished, so hurrying into the passage outside we put on our cloaks and slipped our feet into pattens.

"Hopper hasn't come to work this morning," commented Effie, buttoning up her cloak.

"Perhaps he's ill," I suggested.

"More likely gone for a soldier," she replied.

We went outside to the waiting cart and climbed up. Danny was already sat at the back, swinging his legs over the tail-board, grinning beneath his battered hat. He looked for all the world as if he was off to the fair.

Hugh appeared from the direction of the byre.

"Christmas isn't coming," he called.

"Fancy getting drunk at a time like this," said Effie indignantly.

"He's sleeping it off in the hay-loft."

Hugh clambered up into the driver's seat.

"Not much you can do."

We set off. Effie was in one of her nervous moods, biting her lip, clasping and unclasping her hands. I began to wish she had not come.

Charity Farm was situated on the edge

of the parish of Golding Parva, on the lane leading to Atherstone. It was not the usual sort of farm owned or tenanted by a farmer and his family. Many years ago a local parishioner, one Samuel Jee, had bequeathed the farm to the church, with the instruction that the profit was to pay for a school for the children of Golding Parva and Golding Magna. An excellent idea which had worked well for half a century. The vicar administered the trust, chose the tenants, paid them a wage, kept control of expenditure, and each year handed over the profit to the school.

Unfortunately a problem had arisen. It was found that extensive repairs were required to the school building due to a structural fault, and the money available became insufficient to meet this demand. The present tenants, Mr. and Mrs. Jack Shakespeare, had suggested barn dances run for profit, to help swell the funds available.

It had turned out to be a successful venture; the Charity Farm barn dances became popular over a wide area; and people came from as far afield as Baddesley Ensor. What could be better after a hard day's toil than the music from a couple of fiddles, a few casks of ale, and a willing partner. Many a romance that had blossomed at Charity Farm had later been blessed by the vicar.

As we turned into the yard at Charity Farm I was surprised to see the number that had turned up. I suppose I had the feeling that a dairymaid who had failed to return home after a dance would not arouse much interest. But I had been wrong. There was a silk weaver from Hartshill, a groom from the castle, a ploughman from Hoar Farm, and a shepherd from Hastilow's. They stood about the yard in wide-brimmed dark hats and Bedford cords, armed with rakes or pitchforks, a cheerful, purposeful expression on their faces.

There was also Mrs. Dagley from the turnpike cottage. I was not surprised to see her. That woman had the reputation of being the biggest gossip this side of

Atherstone. Her nose was twitching with excitement, smelling a scandal.

"Well, we've all got to help," she announced, walking across as we climbed down from the cart. "More hands make light work, or something like that."

She was smartly dressed in a new red cloak. Poor Mr. Dagley.

Constable Nat Trye appeared from the farmhouse and strode briskly across to the volunteers, towering above everyone. A big muscular man with a mass of thick black hair and bushy side-whiskers. Not surprisingly he assisted the local blacksmith when not engaged in constable duties.

He looked up at the dark threatening clouds overhead.

"Looks like rain's on the way, folks. Well, we'd best be moving off, and we're going to take the route we think this young woman took to get home. But first I want to search these outbuildings. You can't be too sure of anything."

This was his big day. Not much happened as a rule, a bit of poaching and drunken brawls completed the criminal picture of the Goldings.

We wandered through barns, prodded haystacks, and someone caused such a disturbance in the henhouse, Jack Shakespeare could stand it no longer.

"You're wasting your time," he shouted from the back door. "There ain't no Rose Boultbee here."

And to make matters worse he let his vicious-looking bulldog off the chain.

We left soon after that, walking along the lane in solemn twos, like pilgrims without a shrine, Nat Trye leading, and behind him came the silk weaver and the castle groom, then Mrs. Dagley and Hugh (an ill-matched pair I thought, Hugh looked bored to tears), behind them came the ploughman and the shepherd, then Effie and I, with Danny bringing up the rear.

At the turnpike we turned left. The afternoon stage to Birmingham passed, rattling at a good speed, crowded as usual. Some comic on top shouted indistinguishable ribaldry which made his companions laugh.

We turned down the drive to Red House Farm—a three-storied, red-brick farmhouse set back from the road with a pretty garden in front. There was no trace of Rose, and the farmer and his wife, a pleasant couple and eager to help, had seen no one on the night of the dance.

Back onto the turnpike and a couple of hundred yards ahead on the wide grassy verge beside the road was a gypsy encampment. Despite the fact no gypsy had ever harmed them, fear and hatred rippled through our party as we approached the dirty tents that had been erected around a badly smouldering fire.

Sitting on their haunches by the fire were two women, their dark hair protruding from their turbans, gold earrings dangling from their ears. They were busily engaged making baskets, whilst four ragged children played chase in the tall fox-tail grass behind the tents.

"Where are your men?" Nat demanded of the women.

They shrugged their shoulders. If they knew, they would not have told.

"Either of you seen a young girl Tuesday night coming from Charity Farm?"

"We ain't seen nobody," said one.

The other spit.

"You gypos are born liars. I'm having a look in your tents."

Anger made Nat lose his fear of them. He stepped forward and peered into the interiors of the three tents. He was the only one with the courage to do it. The rest would not have done it for a king's ransom. There was a curse on gypsies. Father said it was because they had made the nails for Christ's cross at Calvary.

"What would these people want with Rose?" Hugh asked in an exasperated tone. "We're wasting time."

"You're forgetting gypsies steal children," the silk weaver reminded him. "So why not Rose—she's not more than a child herself."

Hugh did not look convinced.

Nat rejoined us, shaking his head.

"She's not here."

It started to rain, a steady heavy downpour. We moved on, following the turnpike as it swung round the bend and down to Golding Parva where the church stood in the hollow on the banks of the Bourne—serene and at peace.

The Bourne flowed between the turnpike and the church, and a footpath followed the little river as it meandered through meadows and copses to the mill. Rose would have taken this path. Nat suggested that a few of us walk along the river-bank and the rest fan out in a line across the fields.

"Don't forget," he called. "Anything unusual or suspicious."

I found myself walking along the river-bank with Mrs. Dagley and Effie. We prodded the thick hawthorn bushes that clung to the bank, and kept a sharp watch on the river as it flowed swiftly over the white and brown pebbles. Sometimes a trout darted and was gone.

Mrs. Dagley was in a bad mood.

"That bulldog at Charity Farm nipped me, you know, and I had no idea we were going to that gypsy encampment. Did you see those dirty gypsy women?" She shuddered.

Then a small catastrophe struck.

"Effie!" Mrs. Dagley yelled. "Just look what you've done to my new cloak. You splashed through that puddle and covered it in mud."

"I'm sorry, Mrs. Dagley," mumbled Effie. "It was an accident. I wasn't looking where I was going."

"You call it an accident. I call it something else. My cloak's ruined. I wish I'd never come."

I walked on, not wishing to hear any more. There was a sharp bend in the river, and here the water ceased to flow swiftly and lay dark and deep beneath the gloom of high overhanging banks of holly, the red berries hanging like drops of blood amongst the leaves.

A sudden chill ran through me, like a premonition, and I felt sick, sick with fear. Mrs. Dagley appeared, with Effie following, a crestfallen expression on her face. The three of us stood a moment in that cheerless spot, then breaking an alder branch I prodded the river-bed.

There was nothing there.

Effie plucked my arm nervously.

"Let's go home," she begged me.

"Look, there's Tim O'Reilly's cottage," I said, trying hard to be cheerful. "Let's call on him."

It appeared the rest of the party had the same idea, for we all converged at about the same time on the little tumbled-down place near the river-bank—the men standing in a tight group, the rain pouring from their hats like rivulets.

The cottage had been abandoned by Oarbury farm; the owner, Mr. Ruddle, considered it too dangerous for habitation. The roof was in danger of imminent collapse. Bits of rag filled the places where windows had once been, and ivy almost smothered it, rising up the walls and completely covering the heavily sagging roof.

Tim was an old Irish labourer.

Rheumatism and old age prevented him from working. A couple of years ago he had appeared in the district and one night moved into the old cottage, and remained there ever since. He now appeared in the doorway, holding his ragged cloak close to him, a battered old hat pulled down over his brow, beneath the brim of which his old blue eyes lit up at the prospect of company.

"Ah, sure 'tis a bad day for ye to be taking a stroll. Would you be coming in for a bit?"

"No thanks, Tim, there's too many of us." Nat leaned against Tim's doorway and took a pinch of snuff. "Actually we're here on serious business."

"I swear to God there isn't a rabbit in the place."

He lied with such ease I almost envied him.

"I'm not here for poaching," Nat continued. "I'll see you about that another time. It's about the dairymaid from Dordon's Mill. Did you see her

Tuesday night? She would have passed this way on her way home."

"Dairymaid?" he repeated slowly, wrinkling his brow.

"Rose Boultbee," added Nat. "You must remember her."

"Rose! To be sure I remember her." And the old man's eyes lit up. "Why didn't you say so before. That colleen has hair the colour of moonlight, and eyes as blue as the lakes of Killarney. Sometimes she's after taking pity on an old man and brings me a bit of cheese."

"Never mind about that—did you see her Tuesday night?" Nat repeated.

"Which day be Tuesday, they're all the same to me."

Nat took a deep breath.

"Listen, Tim. Today is Thursday, yesterday was Wednesday, the day before that—Tuesday, Right? We want to know about the day before yesterday."

"The day before yesterday," Tim repeated, looking worried.

"Yes, did you see Rose the day before

yesterday?" A note of impatience had crept into Nat's voice.

"I've seen Rose," he said slowly. "But I don't remember which day."

Nat banged his hands to his side in exasperation.

"Were she with a man?" asked Mrs. Dagley hopefully.

A small light pierced the darkness of Tim's mind and he smiled.

"She said she was meeting one—a gentleman she said."

"Which day was it, Tim?" Nat almost bounced on the old man.

"Did she give the name of the gentleman?" asked the castle groom.

Tim turned in bewilderment from one to the other.

"You'll never get it out of him," called the ploughman. "He's soaked in poteen half the time."

Then Tim's expression of bewilderment turned to one of delight.

"I remember now. It was the day I dug myself a few taters. Mr. Ruddle, he says to me, Tim, if you be wanting a few taters, I wouldn't be after missing a few."

"Come on, let's go," interrupted Nat. "We've wasted enough time here."

And he strode angrily away. The men, Mrs. Dagley and Effie hurried after him.

Tim stood in his doorway, a pathetic expression on his face.

"No one wants you when you're old," he said.

I gave him a copper. It would be spent within the hour at the nearest alehouse, but that was his affair.

I caught up with our little procession, and Mrs. Dagley moved to my side. Her good spirits had returned.

"Who do you think the gentleman was she was meeting."

She twitched her nose.

"I'd give a lot to know that," she continued with relish. "I'll see what Constable Trye thinks."

She hurried on.

"It seems a fruitless afternoon," commented Hugh, stopping to wait for me.

"It certainly is," I agreed.

"You know, Mary, so far we have concentrated on looking for Rose. I'm starting to wonder about Hopper."

"What do you mean?"

"I don't know really. But don't you think it a bit odd that they are both missing?"

"Hopper isn't missing. It's just that he's had too much to drink, and made himself ill. He's done it before."

I always protected Hopper. It was instinctive. He had worked at the mill since he was twelve, and was almost a member of the family like Effie. No, Hopper was not mixed up in this. Yet, I had to admit, it was taking him a long time to recover from his bout of drunkenness.

The rain continued incessantly. What a wet, bedraggled procession we made as we climbed the stile that led into our fields, slipping and squelching along the muddy banks of the leat, with wet clothes and wet feet adding to our misery.

Father was standing in the open

doorway of the mill as we came down the steps and walked in single file across the bridge that spanned the tail-race.

"Any news?" he asked.

"I'm afraid not, Mr. Dordon," called Nat. "We're going in Golding Wood and then that's the finish."

"About time too," exclaimed father. "Wild-goose chase, that's what it is."

We quickened our pace with renewed hearts. Not much further to go now. We crossed the lane, opened the gate, and started climbing the gentle slope of our little valley, taking the footpath across the fields that would lead us to the wood crowning the ridge to the south-west.

The rain started to ease off, and the late afternoon sun made a valiant attempt to break through the heavy blanket of clouds.

At the stile half-way, I paused. Would this dreadful day never end?

We entered the wood, that damp earthy smell filling our nostrils, spreading out in a long line, stumbled through the undergrowth of hazel, dogwood, and bramble.

Thorns plucked at our mud-stained clothes, scratched our hands and faces.

We reached the part of the wood where the ferns grew, now turned to richest bronze, thick as a frothing sea, and in the late afternoon light the colour seemed to deepen and grow more lustrous.

As we proceeded the ferns grew higher, until we were wading through them almost waist-high, and the trees were oak, ancient, gnarled oak. There was a silence in the wood, such a strange silence, as if all the birds had decided not to sing. And then suddenly we saw her—Rose, beautiful Rose—amongst the ferns. She was lying on her back, and her hands were clasped together upon her breast holding a posy of wild flowers. A small branch of oak had been made into a crown and placed upon her head, and winds had sprinkled her with the gilded leaves of autumn.

She was naked, and she was dead.

8

THE men took off their hats, and we stood there stunned, white-faced, in silence for a few minutes, my mind searching for a prayer that would not come. A raindrop rolled slowly down her cheek.

"I think the ladies ought to go home, and I thank them for coming." Nat's voice sounded strained and unnatural.

I turned away, and Mrs. Dagley and Effie followed, through the tall ferns between the oaks, through the sad silent wood in the fading light, down through Mozey's Meadow, and Scott's Rough. And all the time I was thinking of Rose, of her innocence, and how unshakable her belief had been that you could get what you wanted from life.

Who would want to kill her in such bizarre circumstances? Who would want to kill her at all? Rose, who had never done anyone any harm. Who could hate her so much he wanted her dead? There was no answer to these questions.

"Fancy her not having any clothes on," commented Mrs. Dagley as she raised her mud-stained cloak to her fat knees in order to climb the stile. "I mean, not even her stays."

We reached the lane and stood a moment in front of the mill. Work had now ceased for the day; the wheel hung motionless, water still dripping from the floats. I thought of Christmas, and the agonising task of telling him the news.

"I can't wait to tell my Isaac," called Mrs. Dagley cheerfully, her wooden pattens clattering as she crossed the footbridge over the Bourne.

She would not be able to wait until she had told the whole of Gospel Oak, Golding Parva and Golding Magna.

We entered the millhouse to find Father sitting on the settle contentedly smoking his customary evening pipe in the firelight, the mill tabby washing herself at his feet. I was sorry to shatter such a peaceful scene.

"Rose is dead," I said in a flat, dispirited voice.

"Dead!" He jumped to his feet, an angry expression on his face.

"And not a stitch on her," added Effie, as we took off our wet cloaks. "Lying amongst the ferns she was, holding some flowers."

There was silence for a moment, then he said in a thoughtful way:

"Same as Alice Tull."

"It's been a terrible day, Mr. Dordon." Effie put a log upon the fire. "I just can't believe it."

Father stood up and knocked out his pipe.

"I suppose nobody's told Christmas?"

I shook my head.

"I'd better go and do it." He tightened his lips. "Get it over with. Do you know where he is?"

"You'll probably find him still in the hayloft."

He moved towards the door.

"How did she die?" he asked, softly.

"I don't know. I expect Nat will be telling us."

He went into the kitchen, and shortly after we heard the back door close behind him. Effie sat down on the settle. Her hands were shaking badly.

"It's put my nerves on edge, Mary. I keep thinking of Christmas. It'll finish him. There was nobody as good as his Rose. Well, I'll have to get a meal ready. I couldn't eat a thing myself, but your father will be hungry."

She went into the kitchen, and I lingered for a while by the fire. I think I was in a state of shock. I felt exhausted.

I could hear Effie making up the fire in the kitchen and filling the kettle with water, and I began to be conscious of the empty dairy down the passage where Rose would never churn butter again, nor make the cheese. She would never smile again, nor put her arm through mine. Confide her dreams, her hopes. I lit the candle and put it on the table.

It started to rain, and the wind flung

the raindrops angrily against the window. A loose shutter banged against the outside wall. It seemed to catch a raw nerve. After a while I could stand it no longer, and went outside and secured it. The light had almost gone from the sky and my eyes were drawn like a magnet to Golding Wood. A light danced amongst its trees. Nat must still be in there with the volunteers. I shivered.

As I re-entered the parlour, to my astonishment I heard the sound of sobbing coming from the kitchen, and on hurrying in found Effie, a crumpled figure by the window, weeping. I rushed to her and crouched by her side.

"Effie, don't distress yourself so. It's been a nightmare, I know."

I stroked her grey head.

"I said she'd run away with a soldier." Effie buried her face in her hands. "It was a dreadful thing to say."

"Not really," I said, trying to console her.

"Oh, Mary, you know as well as I do girls who run away with soldiers usually become a camp whore. And I said that about her! I'll never forgive myself. I was jealous of her youth and beauty. That surprises you, doesn't it, Mary?"

She burst into a fresh paroxysm of weeping.

The kettle began to boil, and I made a pot of tea.

When her weeping subsided, Effie took off her spectacles and wiped them.

"You must think I'm just a stupid old woman."

"I don't think anything of the sort. Its a brave woman who confesses her weaknesses."

I handed her a cup of tea.

"Thanks, Mary. I'm glad you're home. And I hope you're going to be here for a very long time."

"I am, Effie. Now drink the tea while it's hot."

She sipped the tea contentedly, and when she finished she gave me a grave smile.

"I'll try to keep myself under better control in future."

We started making preparations for the supper. Strange, I mused, as I peeled the potatoes, that Alice and Rose were both found murdered in the wood, and in the same circumstances, naked and holding flowers. Obviously the work of the same madman. I found myself wishing Harry was home. I had the feeling if he was here everything would be all right.

A sudden hammering at the door startled me. Effie looked up from her baking in a panic, putting her hands to her head.

"I can't stand much more today, Mary. Will you go and see who it is?"

I went through to the parlour and opened the door. To my surprise Nat Trye was standing there, with Danny, Hugh, and Nicholas Jeffcoate.

"Could I have a word with you, Mary, and your father, if he's about? Just a few questions."

"Certainly, Nat. Come in."

The four men walked into the parlour. Nicholas barely smiled at me.

"Father's in the byre talking to Christmas. Please sit down."

I indicated the chairs round the dining-table.

They sat down, an aura of gloom surrounding them.

"Effie, will you bring in a jug of ale," I called as I went to the dresser and took down the tankards.

"Thanks, Mary," said Nat. "We could do with a drop of summat." There was a flicker of interest round the table. "It's been a bad business." He continued unbuttoning his jacket. "Doctor Jeffcoate here has just examined the body. Lucky we met him at the village."

Nat looked tired and worried. Up to a few hours ago it was just a case of a dairy-maid who had failed to come home from a barn dance. Now it was murder. I could see he regretted taking up the duties of village constable last summer. Nicholas appeared to be studying the surface of the polished table, Hugh was gazing pensively at the tapestry map, but Danny smiled happily round the table, feeling pleased with himself. He had never been asked to sit on Mr. Dordon's chairs before.

"What was the cause of death?" I asked as Effie poured out the ale.

"A knife through the heart," said Nicholas, looking up. "I found the wound when I removed the flowers."

"We're looking for that knife," added Nat.

Father was taking so long, I thought, as I handed round the tankards, I began to wonder if I should go out to the byre to fetch him. Then the kitchen door opened, and he stood there, pausing in the doorway, to survey the visitors.

"Evening everyone."

"How's Christmas?" I asked, afraid of the answer. Father shook his head.

"He's taken it bad. I knew he would. Worse job I've had to do in my life."

There was a painful silence.

Then Nat drained his tankard in one go and wiped his mouth with the back of his hand.

"I needed that. Now I've got to ask a few questions. I've got to have all my facts afore I sees Sir Francis. You know what he's like."

Sir Francis was one of the toughest magistrates in this part of Warwickshire, and woe betide any constable who fell short of his duties.

"I want to find out who Rose was with Tuesday night," Nat continued. "Tim O'Reilly says she told him she was meeting a gentleman. Which day that was we can never be sure. We can only assume it were Tuesday until we know otherwise. Anyone know of a gentleman who's courting a dairymaid?"

An uneasy laughter rippled round the table.

"Now I want to know where you all was Tuesday night. I've had satisfactory answers from those what were with us this afternoon, and I'll be asking this question tomorrow to everybody who knew her."

A flicker of uneasiness stirred through the room, like a breeze stirring the summer barley. It was very gentle, but it was there.

"Of course I can't ask such a question to a learned man like yourself, Dr. Jeffcoate, you would consider it an impertinence."

"Not at all," replied Nicholas casually, but in the candle-light his face looked gaunt. "I'll tell you exactly where I was. I was at home all evening cataloguing my butterflies."

I gazed at Nicholas in astonishment. His horse and gig had been in the lane that night. Effie had been too intoxicated to notice anything, but Father had seen it. I looked across at him for his reaction. His face was completely expressionless. Was he protecting Nicholas?

"Now, Mr. Dordon," said Nat. "Where were you that night?"

"That's easy. I was invited to Hugh's cottage to his birthday celebration. Mary and Effie came with me."

"That right, Mr. Morganwy?"

"Of course," Hugh reassured him. "They were with me all evening."

"And you did not see Rose that evening?"

"No," he replied.

"That's four of you accounted for already."

Nat started to relax.

"Now, Danny, where were you that night?"

Danny did not answer. He was staring at the polished brass face of the Cromwell clock. Anything that shone always fascinated him.

"Danny, stop looking at that clock. Where were you Tuesday night?" Nat repeated.

There was still no reply from him.

Then Nat lost his temper. He had neither the patience nor understanding to deal with a mentally retarded young man.

"Answer me, you dumb idiot. You tell me where you were Tuesday night, otherwise it will be the worse for you." And he raised his clenched fist at him. "Rose Boultbee's been murdered, and I'm going to find out who done it."

The sight of Nat's clenched fist wrought panic in Danny. He obviously could not understand why Nat was asking him questions at all.

"I ain't done nothing. I never touched her. Hopper said I wasn't to drink ale, and I never did."

He stood up, his hands trembling, beads of perspiration standing out on his forehead.

"I ain't done nothing. I ain't killed Rose."

Then like a cornered animal desperate for escape he made a rush for the door. But Nat was too quick for him. He sprang across the room and grabbed his arm.

"Oh no you don't. You're not leaving this room until you've answered my questions."

"Answer him, Danny," I begged. "Just say you went to the barn dance."

But he would not listen.

"I ain't killed Rose," he kept repeating.

"You won't get any sense out of him while he's in this mood," advised Father. "I suggest you leave him until tomorrow when he's calmed down. He's had a bad experience. He liked Rose."

Nat flung the door open.

"You haven't heard the last of this," he barked.

Delighted to be free, Danny rushed out into the night.

Nat walked slowly back to his seat.

"I don't seem to be getting anywhere," he said wearily, sitting down.

There was silence for a few moments, then he said:

"Has anybody any idea who Rose's gentleman friend was?"

None of us knew.

"She never mentioned anyone," said Father. "And she was a very talkative sort of girl. I'm surprised at this because I thought Hopper was courting her."

"Did she go to the dance with Hopper?" asked Nat, looking interested.

"She was seen at the dance with him," I ventured.

"Now we're getting somewhere. Hopper and Rose were sweethearts."

"Not exactly," I said. "Danny told me they quarrelled at the dance. Then Rose went home alone. He saw her running down the lane."

Nat's eyes gleamed.

"A lover's quarrel, and afterwards she ran away from the dance. Hopper followed her and murdered her."

"That's ridiculous," I exclaimed angrily. "Hopper loved Rose."

"All the more reason for wanting to murder her. She'd found herself another lover—this gentleman. Where is Hopper by the way?"

Nat looked round.

"I haven't seen him since Tuesday evening when he finished work," replied Father in an irritated tone. "Two days now he hasn't turned up, and he knows it's our busy season. Those barn dances are a menace."

"Where does he live?"

I did not like the tone of Nat's voice.

"Come on! What's his address?"

No one wanted to play Judas. Not to dear silly Hopper. Breaking his heart over Rose. Getting drunk over Rose. If only he had come to work and been here to defend himself. Now he was in trouble. The biggest trouble of his life.

"If you don't tell me, someone at the Wheatsheaf will."

"Applepie Lane, going Atherstone way." Father spoke in a quiet, resigned voice. I knew Hopper annoyed him sometimes, but he liked the boy, and wished him no harm.

"I'll be down Applepie Lane in the morning." Nat stood up, looking pleased with himself. "That is after I've seen Sir Francis. And my guess is he'll think the same as me, and young Hopper's going to end up at Warwick Assizes. What do you say, Doctor Jeffcoate?"

Nicholas gave him a guarded look.

"I can't give an opinion," he replied. "But I would advise him to get a good lawyer."

"He'll need that all right," laughed Nat. "Well, thank you all for your help."

There was a scraping of chairs as the men rose to their feet. Suddenly the sound of crashing crockery came from the kitchen, and Christmas staggered in, extremely drunk. The look in his eyes frightened me, and as he reached up for Father's gun over the ingle-nook Nat and Hugh leapt forward and held him by the arms.

"I'll kill the bastard," he cried. "Let me have that pistol."

"Take hold of yourself, Christmas," warned Nat. "Don't do anything you'll be sorry for."

He struggled for a moment, then seemed to crumple like a piece of paper, sobbing like a child.

"Rose! What they done to you, and you weren't even decent!"

The two men eased him into a chair. "Don't you worry, Christmas," Nat consoled him. "We know who done it and he'll swing for it."

"And I know too. It were that bastard Danny. Stands to reason don't it, only a madman would do a thing like that. And he's mad all right. I seen him once. Dancing he was. All by himself in the dark up in Mozey's Meadow."

"I'm seeing Sir Francis tomorrow,"

continued Nat. "But my suspicions lie in another direction."

Effie handed Christmas her pocket handkerchief. Her face was full of compassion.

"If there's anything I can do, Christmas."

"Thanks, Effie." He blew his nose. "There ain't anything anyone can do, except get the bastard what done it."

"Come on, Christmas. I'll take you home in the cart," said Father, walking across to him. "Get a good night's rest and you'll feel better tomorrow." And taking the old man firmly by the arm he guided him out into the night.

Nat, Hugh and Nicholas followed. I stood at the door watching them go, then returning to the fireside sat down with Effie to await Father's return. He was back within the hour, his face tired and strained.

"I don't think we'll have any cows milked in the morning," he said as we sat down to the late supper.

"I can milk, Mr. Dordon," announced

Effie. "I used to milk the cow my father kept."

"Thanks, Effie."

I could eat little, and Effie was not eating at all. I looked across at her and her lips were trembling, tears were very near.

"They can't hang Hopper," she said. "Not Hopper. I keep thinking of him when he first came here. Such a small boy, and so shy."

I was thinking of Hopper too. Tomorrow he would be on his way to Warwick Gaol, and the thought of it filled me with horror.

"If someone warned Hopper tonight," I suggested, "he could run away to a place of safety."

"Don't talk daft." Father looked at me angrily. "If Hopper is innocent he has nothing to fear. If he runs away tonight, he'll be on the run for the rest of his life. Now keep out of it, Mary. Leave things be. Justice will prevail."

I was not so sure. My trust in human

nature had gone. I felt distrustful and suspicious of everyone.

"I can't help agreeing with Christmas about Danny," Father continued. "I always feel there's an underlying sense of violence in the fellow. It's just that we handle him with kindness so it's never really come to the surface."

I had seen it come to the surface, I thought, the night I had arrived and found him in Father's room. And then I thought of yesterday when he had admitted he had followed Rose when she had run down the lane. She had told him to go away. Had it made Danny angry, and he had in fact continued following her, and then killed her?

"How I'd like to lay my hands on that murderer," exclaimed Father angrily. "I'd throttle him with my own hands."

I hated to see Father in this mood.

"Why don't you do a bit of carving," I suggested. "That swallow will never be finished."

"Good idea, Mary. Help me to forget this business, if only for a short time."

He walked across to the cupboard beneath the dresser and took out the half-completed swallow.

"Nothing like a bit of carving to sooth the troubled spirit." A cheerful note crept into his voice. "When I've finished it, I think I'll give it to Grace. She's been good to you, Mary." Then he knelt down at the cupboard again, a perplexed expression on his face. "Where's my knife?" he exclaimed. "I always keep it in this cupboard. It's gone."

9

"IT must be there. I'll have a look."

Kneeling down I examined the contents of the dresser cupboard. It was filled with Father's miscellaneous personal belongings: Interesting pieces of wood for future carvings, hammers, a set of files, a box of nails, spare pipes, tinder-boxes, sealing wax, a box containing tobacco. The knife was not there.

"I have a small knife in the kitchen that might be suitable," Effie suggested. "Just you see when spring-cleaning time comes I'll find it."

"But I always keep it in this cupboard."

Father was clearly mystified.

Effie hurried into the kitchen and returned with a small knife.

"Use it until you find your own. They do say, when you've lost something, hang a rabbit's paw over your bed."

"Give it to me, Effie," he said exasperatedly, taking the knife from her. He ran his finger delicately along the blade.

"Thanks, Effie. It'll do." His tone was begrudging. "But it's not as good as the old un."

The rain continued through the night. I did not sleep well. I never do when I'm unhappy, and my dreams were filled with anxiety and fear. The old feeling of security had gone.

I awoke next morning to the sound of heavy rain stabbing against the window, and wondered if Nat Trye was already on his way to Hopper's cottage. I got out of bed, and on looking through the window to my dismay saw the Bourne was in flood. Where it had crossed the lane yesterday a stream about ten feet wide, now it was a rushing torrent, trebled in size. How fortunate the mill-house had been built on a sufficient rise, which kept the water at bay, at least for the time being.

Father was in the parlour lighting a lantern.

"I'm not taking any chances," he said as I walked in. "Everything comes out of the cellar."

I smiled to myself. Father was a born worrier. It was six years since the mill had been flooded.

"It's a long time since I've seen it so wide."

He said this every year.

"I'll help you, Father."

The entrance to the cellar was in the parlour, directly beneath the stairs. Father opened the door, and to my surprise the delicate scent of apples filled my nostrils.

"I didn't know you stored apples down here," I said as I followed him down, the lantern casting a yellow pool of light on the worn stone steps.

"We had such a good crop of apples this year," Father explained as we descended. "I didn't know where to store them all. That is, where they'd be free from mice. Then I had this idea."

We had now reached the bottom of the steps. In the lantern light I saw he had suspended wooden trays from the cellar ceiling by short lengths of rope, and onto each section of rope he had threaded a disc of wood, several inches in diameter.

He pointed to the discs.

"That stops the little varmints. You see they comes down the rope and when they gets to these here discs, it flummoxes them. They run round and round on it, and when they're fed up with that, they go back up the rope."

Father looked so pleased at his triumph over mice. His life was one long battle against the little creatures.

I had not been in the cellar for years, and as Father held the lantern up there was something different about the place.

"You've cleaned the walls."

"Effie did that in September. She said if apples are going to be stored down here she wanted the place clean. She scrubbed them walls. Do you remember them? They were filthy. Your mother would never use this place. She hated it. She always had a fear of the dark," he added softly.

I shared my mother's fear of the dark, and to make matters worse, as a child Christmas had told me the cellar was haunted by the "old man of the mill". "The old man" being a statue in the cellar which he swore came alive at night. Grandfather had found it when digging the foundations for the dairy extension. The womenfolk had taken a dislike to it, and it had been put in the cellar, remaining there ever since. A childish fear still lingered at the edge of my mind.

"Is the statue still here?" I ventured.

"It's still here," replied Father in a disinterested tone. "One day I'll get rid of it."

We walked down to the end of the cellar, and he shone his lantern on it.

It was a strange, crude statue, finishing at the waist, black with dirt, the face flat, the features roughly carved, and the ears were too large for the head.

"I might be able to get a few bob for it at Atherstone market," he remarked. "Well, let's set to work."

One by one we unhooked the trays of

apples and took them upstairs to the dairy.

"Better be safe than sorry," he said as we placed them on the thrawl.

We returned to the cellar for the last tray. The light from the lantern swept across the face of the statue, and for a brief, illuminating moment it looked alive.

"Will you sell that statue, Father?" I urged. "I know it's silly of me, but I do dislike it so."

"Don't tell me you still take notice of what Christmas says. Well, I'll get rid of it just as soon as I get the time."

We put the last tray in the dairy.

"I suppose there's no news of Hopper?" I asked.

"None. Oh, speaking of Hopper—I've got a memory like a sieve. It's him I lent the knife to. I suppose I'll get it back one of these days. And where are you off today?"

"Another music lesson at the castle," I replied enthusiastically. "Before I go I must write out a little tune for Caroline to learn."

"Mind how you go," he cautioned me. "Remember the murderer still hasn't been caught. Speak to no one."

"I'll remember, Father."

I went up to my room, and on a spare sheet of paper wrote a simple tune, then putting on my cloak, went down to the kitchen, where, to my surprise, Effie was sat by the fire repairing a rip in one of Christmas's shirts.

Seeing my look of surprise, she blushed a little.

"An act of atonement you might say." She spoke in a self-conscious manner. "For what I said about Rose."

"You're a good woman, Effie," I said, giving her a hug.

"Did you do the milking this morning?"

"No. Christmas did it. He's not as irresponsible as your father thinks."

Effie was changing.

There was no abatement in the rain, and the ever-swelling Bourne was creeping nearer to the mill. To avoid the flooding, I turned the pony's head in the direction of Golding Parva.

It was a cold, penetrating rain, and I sat huddled over the reins in a troubled mood. So many things worried me. Father had lent his knife to Hopper. Hopper was missing, and Rose had been murdered with a knife. Was it time I ceased to protect him, and realise the possibility that Hopper might have something to hide?

And why had Nicholas Jeffcoate lied to Nat about his whereabouts on Tuesday night? I could find no answer to that, and as regards Danny, he was capable of murder. The mind of a child in the body of a man, with all a man's natural instincts. It was possible.

I entered the courtyard of the castle. Suddenly I remembered with a shock Charles would have been in Golding Wood on Tuesday night. He had said he had waited at the stile, and through the wood was the quickest way back to

Golding Castle. The thought of it made me tense.

How I wished life could be simple, I thought, as Lotty let me in, and I made my way along the passage to Aunt Grace's sitting-room. The room was empty, and feeling sure she would not mind I took off my wet cloak and hung it behind her door, then made my way to the music-room.

As I opened the door the loveliness of the room greeted me; the rich colours in the carpets, the glitter of the chandelier, the warm glow of the mahogany.

I walked across to the pianoforte, put my sheet of music on the stand, then idly strummed my fingers on the keys, and for a moment I was happy.

I did not have to wait long, for as the little clock gently chimed the hour the door opened and Caroline walked into the room. She made such a pretty figure in her yellow gown, flaxen ringlets, and white frilly pantaloons reaching to her ankles. But as she approached I noticed her face was tear-stained.

"Oh, Miss Dordon, I'm so glad you're here. I was afraid you might not come."

"Why shouldn't I come? Is there anything wrong, Caroline?" I asked, feeling concerned.

She did not answer and looked sheepishly away.

"Where's Jamie?"

"As he's not learning the pianoforte, Miss Plum is giving him an arithmetic lesson. He'll like that."

Tears appeared in her eyes, and she hastily brushed them away.

"Tell me what's happened," I asked as gently as I could. "Perhaps I could help you."

"Nobody can help me. You see, when I had my music lesson on Wednesday Jamie broke a piece of china. He took it out of grandmother's cabinet."

She indicated the large glass cabinet further down the room filled with Chelsea china.

"I wouldn't even touch a piece of grandmother's china, and he told Miss Plum I had broken it."

I looked into her earnest little face and instinctively felt she was telling the truth.

"I hope you told Miss Plum that was not true."

Caroline nodded.

"She won't believe me and she's going to punish me."

More tears appeared in her blue eyes. It was obviously a catastrophy of alarming proportions to Caroline.

"Sometimes I feel like running away."

"You mustn't do that, Caroline."

I decided it was time to start the lesson. "Sit down on the stool and let me hear you play the five-finger exercise."

Caroline sat down on the stool and demonstrated how well she had learnt her first lesson. Then I pointed to the music on the stand.

"Now, Caroline, I have here a simple tune you can learn to play for your father before he returns to his regiment. If you learn it well, he will be so pleased."

Her tears were forgotten, and she gave an excited laugh.

"Place your fingers on the keyboard, and let's see if you can find the notes."

She started learning the tune, slowly note by note, first with the right hand and then with the left.

"Now we'll do the two hands together." She struggled through the piece, striking the occasional wrong note.

"Not too bad for the first try," I said encouragingly. "Now again."

This time she was a little better, and feeling more confident, she sang the words in a thin, clear voice:

"Ring a ring a roses,
A pocket full of posies,
Atishu, atishu,
We all fall down."

We all fall down. First Alice, and then Rose. Who would be next? I glanced towards the window. It had stopped raining and the sun was breaking through the clouds, glittering the leaves on the boxwood hedge outside the window.

"Miss Dordon," said Caroline. "A dairymaid's been murdered."

"How did you know?"

"I heard the maids talking. They say the idiot boy at the mill did it."

"I think it best if we don't talk about it. You see, Rose was a friend of mine."

"Oh, I am sorry, Miss Dordon."

"Now let me hear you play 'Ring a ring a roses' again,—and no wrong notes."

Caroline played the tune again and again until there were no wrong notes. Then she stopped, rested her fingers on the keyboard, and looked up at me eagerly:

"Am I good enough to play to Papa?"

I could not resist giving her a hug.

"You certainly are."

She clapped her hands excitedly, then her face darkened.

"I wish you were my governess instead of that horrid Miss Plum. I hate her."

"Now, Caroline. You must not say such things about Miss Plum. She would be most offended if she heard you."

"But it's true," she protested. "She

always punishes me, and never Jamie. Jamie's her favourite."

I held up my hand.

"No more about Miss Plum."

"Miss Dordon . . ."

I looked round to see Lady Eleanor standing in the doorway.

"Is the music lesson finished?"

"Yes, Lady Eleanor. Just this moment."

"Could I have a word with you? Now, Caroline, run along to the schoolroom."

Picking up my sheet of music, we walked across the room to her—a proud, sad-faced woman. I liked her. She was obviously just off for a drive, wearing a warm-looking mantle trimmed with fur. She gave her grandchild an affectionate hug, then the little girl dashed past her and ran quickly across the courtyard.

"Caroline's always in a hurry," she said, watching her, then she turned to me. "Miss Dordon, I can't tell you how pleased I am that she's learning the pianoforte. My favourite instrument. I used to play it, and the harpsichord, a long time ago."

She held up her fingers swollen from arthritis.

"Every age has its compensations. I have my grandchildren." She gave one of her rare smiles. "Such a shame about the broken china," she continued, "but these things happen where there are children." Her tone was light, and she gave the impression of not being particularly concerned.

Behind her in the courtyard the castle phaeton drew up, and from a door in the Elizabethan building Emma Drew emerged—a lovely figure in a crimson gown trimmed with swan's-down and a beaver hat upon her head. She waved to her mother as she walked across to the phaeton.

"There's Emma," exclaimed Lady Eleanor. "I'll have to go. Oh, I nearly forgot. Robert would like to see you in the library. It's nothing to worry about—he's very pleased with you. He might be delayed, I'm afraid, so amuse yourself with the books." She drew on her gloves. "Such a busy day. It's the Tenants' Supper tonight. I presume you will be coming?"

"The Tenants' Supper? Oh yes, of course."

I had completely forgotten about it. It was an annual event, and even though grandfather Dordon had bought the freehold of the mill we were still eligible because father rented Mozey's Meadow from the Drews.

Lady Eleanor walked across to the waiting carriage to join her daughter. I closed the door and crossed the music-room. Charles would think Emma Drew beautiful, I thought, as I climbed the narrow spiralling staircase that led up to the library.

Thinking of Charles was a searing pain. I had not realised it would hurt so badly. When I reached the library, the quiet, relaxing atmosphere, the bright fire burning in the grate, acted as a soothing balm. From the window patches of blue sky were visible. My thoughts turned to the mill. Now that it had stopped raining, there was a chance for the Bourne to recede. Father would be pleased.

I sat down in one of the armchairs before the fire. The translation of Julius Caesar's *De Bello Gallico* still lay open on the little table at my side. Whoever was reading it was still at the same page. Having nothing better to do I started reading—after all Lady Eleanor had given me permission.

The page dealt with Julius Caesar's description of the Druids, a religion that flourished in the British Isles at the time of the Roman invasion in 54 BC:

> They attend to divine worship, perform public and private sacrifices, and expound matters of religion. A great number of youths gather round them for the sake of education, and they enjoy the highest honour in the nation . . .

As I read on I was finding it more and more difficult to sustain my interest.

Finally I replaced it on the little table. As I did so, I noticed more books beneath the table. There was Gibson's edition of *Camden's Britannia*, Stukeley's *Itinerarium Curiosum*, and *History of Celtic Britain* by John Gough. I picked up Gough's history, and turning the pages the following caught my attention:

> The ancient Britons (or Celts) observed the following feast days in their calendar: Samhain on the 1st November, Oimelc on the 1st February, Beltane on the 1st May, and Lugnasad on the 1st August. On these days it was the custom for the Druid priests to offer up human sacrifices to the gods. These sacrifices were performed in oak groves, the oak being regarded by the Druids as a magical tree.

I had a sudden mental picture of Rose lying amongst the oak trees in Golding Wood, a crown of oak leaves upon her head, laid out . . . *like a sacrifice*.

I reeled at the shock.

Then I read the page again, and this time another thought struck me. Rose had been murdered on 1st November, and in the Celtic calendar the 1st November was the feast of Samhain.

Was it a coincidence?

I closed the book; I could read no more, the print was swimming before my eyes.

10

PLACING the book on the little table I leaned back in the armchair and closed my eyes. If I had told anyone my thoughts at that moment they would have considered me quite mad. A Druid murder in the county of Warwickshire in the year 1815! It was of course preposterous, yet at the same time someone in this castle was interested in Druid rituals—the books at my side were evidence of this. And had the same person also performed them?

A sudden chill ran through me.

"Miss Dordon. My apologies."

Robert Drew's voice startled me so I almost jumped. I opened my eyes to find him standing before me, an anxious look upon his face. I made an effort to rise.

"Please be seated. Anything wrong? You don't look at all well."

"I'll be all right, Mr. Drew. It's just the bad news we had yesterday."

"Oh yes. I heard about it from Constable Trye. Your dairymaid was found murdered in Golding Wood. I am sorry, frightening business. And of course one of our maids was murdered there too. Very queer."

He paused, reflecting. I regarded him carefully. Robert Drew was a kind man, and murderers are not kind men. No, I felt sure it was not Robert Drew.

"I wanted to see you about Caroline," he continued. "I heard her practising this morning. She's very eager to learn, and she told me she likes you. I think it's so important that the pupil feels at ease with her instructor. Don't you agree?"

I agreed.

"She's a nervous child, and you seem to have instilled confidence into her. Now I shall be returning to my regiment in a few days, and I don't know when I'll be back. Will you give me your assurance that you will continue the music lessons for at least a year, or until I return? Good teachers like you are hard to find."

Blushing at his compliment, I gave him my assurance.

"I like to go away feeling everything is organised, at least as far as the children are concerned. If any problems arise, see my mother. Well, I think that's all, Miss Dordon. I'll say good-day to you and thank you."

Walking through the great hall and down the steps, with Robert Drew's praise still ringing in my ears, I felt the world was a smiling place again.

I took the corridor that led to the kitchen quarters. Two harassed-looking maids hurried past, and I thought of Alice. She too had once hurried along this same corridor, and suddenly the world was no longer a smiling place but one where a murderer lurked.

I found Aunt Grace in her sitting-room, and as I entered she was in the act of making a pot of tea.

"Come in, Mary," she called cheerfully. "You're just in time."

She set out another cup and saucer.

"I hope you did not mind my leaving my cloak here," I said as I closed the door.

"Mind? Course not. You must always leave it here. Come and sit by the fire. Well, and how are you liking it?"

"I like teaching Caroline very much. She's a bit upset at the moment. She says she was wrongly accused of breaking a piece of her grandmother's china."

Aunt Grace handed me a cup of tea.

"I heard about it. With children it's very difficult to know whether they're lying or not. Though in this case I should say if anybody's been doing any breaking, it's Jamie. He's got that mischievous look. Anyway, it won't happen again." And she touched the keys at her waist. "I've locked up the china cabinets. Should have been done before."

She sat down opposite me.

"Oh, I've just remembered. I have a letter for you."

"A letter? For me?" I exclaimed, surprised.

She went across to a chest of drawers and started rummaging about in the top drawer. "Mr. Field gave it to me. I thought he was here until the weekend because of the Saturday hunt. Anyway, he left suddenly on Wednesday, and before he went he gave me this letter to give to you. I clean forgot about it. I am sorry, Mary, otherwise I would have sent it round with a groom. I've been that rushed off my feet."

She handed me the letter, an anxious look on her face.

"I know it's none of my business, Mary. I'm very fond of you, not having any children of my own, and you being my brother's child. Mr. Field is a very nice gentleman. You can always tell by the way they treat the servants—not like some I know. But you're on dangerous ground. Stands to reason, money marries money. Stick to your own class."

She handed me the letter.

"You have no need to worry, Aunt Grace," I assured her in a level voice.

"Whatever friendship there was between us has now ended."

I put the letter in my gown pocket.

"I'm glad to hear it. Like a piece of cake?"

I took the piece of cake and sipped Aunt Grace's tea.

Would the memory of Charles never cease to hurt?

"Oh, Mary, how time flies. It only seems yesterday when you were a little girl and sitting in that chair, and look at you now, a grown woman." Then her voice took on a sad note. "We heard about Rose last night. Poor Rose, the best always go first, I say. She was a lovely girl, just like Alice."

"Aunt Grace, can you remember which day Alice was murdered?"

"Sometime in the summer—haymaking time I think."

"Try hard. It's important."

There was a long pause as Aunt Grace tried to recollect the events of last summer, then she pursed her lips and frowned.

"It's no good. All I remember was haymaking time. Everybody from the village was out in the fields helping. It was a courting couple left their haymaking and went for a stroll in the wood that found her. That was a terrible day."

"Never mind. It was just an idea I had."

I finished my tea and thanked her.

"Nothing like a cup of tea," she smiled. "I know there's a lot of folks against tea. They say it does terrible things to your inside, but I'll have mine any day."

I took my cloak from behind the door.

"I'll see you tonight at the Tenants' Supper," I said as I put the cloak around my shoulders.

"I'm hoping it will be the best supper ever," she replied. "Well, I'd best be getting back to the kitchen and seeing how those maids are getting on with that Windsor pudding."

I opened the door.

"Lammas Day," she said.

"What do you mean?"

"It was Lammas Day," she repeated, "when Alice was murdered. It's all coming back to me now. We always have a bit of a celebration evening of Lammas Day. You know, a cask or two of ale, bit of dancing. I remember I thought it strange Alice not being there. She loved dancing. Then of course she was found, a bit later on that evening."

I left her surpervising the maids in the kitchen, mounted the pony, and set off down the drive, my mind teeming. Lammas Day was 1st August, and according to the book in the library the 1st August was also the Celtic feast of Lugnasad. Both girls had been murdered on Celtic feast days.

It could not be a coincidence!

Another point in favour of the Celtic festival idea, both deaths were identical. No one would take me seriously, I thought sadly as I rode into Golding Magna village. Nat Trye was standing in the doorway of the Wheatsheaf. I stopped, and he walked across to me.

"Hello, Nat. Any news of Hopper?"

He looked depressed.

"I went to Applepie Lane this morning, but his old mother hasn't seen him since he left for the barn dance Tuesday night. Nobody's seen him. He's as slippery as an eel, that one."

"Have you found the knife that killed Rose?"

"No," he replied gloomily. "That's like looking for a needle in a haystack. If you hear anything, Mary, let me know."

Bidding Nat good-bye, I continued down the village street, a feeling of concern for Hopper gathering within me. If he needed my help, I would give it willingly.

Leaving the village behind, the peaceful countryside spread out before me in an undulating pattern of irregular fields, bordered by hedges and trees, with here and there a red-brick farmhouse surrounded by barns and outbuildings. I suddenly wondered if Hopper was hiding in one of them, cold, frightened, and hungry. There was nothing I could do unless he showed himself.

The lane started to drop down into our little valley, and when the mill came into view I was relieved to see the Bourne had receded a little. A few dry days and it would be back to normal.

Putting the pony in the stable I walked round to the back of the mill. The air smelt clean and sweet after the rain, and the crimson fruit of the guelder rose hung lush and heavy on the bough.

I found Hugh and Danny sat on an old tree-trunk on the banks of the mill-pond, enjoying their midday break. Danny was busy trailing a stick in the water, whilst Hugh sat hugging his knees, a pensive expression on his face.

"I see your thoughts are far away, Hugh," I remarked as I stood before him.

"Mary. I'm so sorry. I didn't see you. Please sit down."

I sat down next to him. He gave me a welcoming smile.

"Yes, I was miles away just then."

"Playing one of those wonderful melodies on the harp."

He smiled. "No. Just thinking of home."

"Where exactly are the Black Mountains?"

"Travel south-west from here until you come to the town of Hereford. Cross the river Wye, and there on the horizon you will see them—dark and grieving. You can go a whole winter and never see the summits—wreathed in clouds they are. Curlew and buzzard breed up there, and there's plenty of red grouse in the autumn. Ah, that's when the heather's in bloom—purple it is, as far as the eye can see. We never saw anyone up there—Father and I. The old legend did that, kept folks away."

"What was the old legend?"

"They said there was an evil spirit in the mountains. Sometimes it took the form of a woman, sometimes a man, and it led travellers to their death. Father and I never minded. We preferred to be alone."

"But didn't you feel lonely, Hugh? Never seeing anyone."

"Once a year we went to Hereford market and sold our sheep. I always enjoyed that day, but when nightfall came I was always glad to get back. It's where I belong. Where my roots are. I felt loneliness for the first time in my life when my father died."

"I hope your stay here will be a very long one. I suppose one day you will return?"

"I suppose so."

"I hope that day is in the distant future. Father seems to rely more and more on you. And I hear it was most fortunate you were here when he was taken ill last summer."

Hugh smiled in an embarrassed way.

"I did my best to help him. He's a good man. Well, I could stay here all day talking to you, Mary. I must go and do some work, and so must Danny. Come on, Danny."

Danny threw his stick away reluctantly, and the three of us started walking back to the mill. I thought he looked most unhappy.

"What's the matter, Danny?"

"Nothing," he replied in a sulky voice.

"Come on, tell me about it," I insisted. "You'll feel better if you do."

"It's Constable Trye," he replied in a worried voice. "I don't like him asking me questions. I ain't done nothing. When's he coming back?"

"I don't know, but when he does, just tell him the truth. On Tuesday night you were at the barn dance. It's quite simple."

Life was unbelievably complicated for Danny. We had now reached the mill. The two men entered the weighing-room and I walked round to the kitchen.

"Your father's just gone to Atherstone," said Effie as she spooned broth into two bowls. "He's hoping to do business with that new baker, and he'll be back in the middle of the afternoon."

We were eating a quick lunch in the parlour when we heard the back door open and Christmas walked into the parlour. He did not look the same man.

Sober, serious, shaven, and wearing a clean shirt.

"I won't be able to make any sheep-dip," he announced. "Arsenic's missing. I always keep it on the same shelf in the byre, and it's gone."

"Well, you must have put it on another shelf," said Effie. "Anyway, what are you worrying about, Christmas? It's six months to sheep-dipping time."

"That ain't the point. There's a thief about, and I don't like it."

"There's no thief here," said Effie indignantly. "You've just mislaid it. That's all."

This did not satisfy Christmas.

"I haven't touched it since last spring," he continued firmly. "Arsenic don't walk off shelves. I knows it was there. Someone's pinched it, and I want to find out who it is."

"I hope you find the culprit," I said, stacking dirty dishes onto the tray. "And when we get a fresh supply, keep it in a different place."

He went out, banging the door behind him, still grumbling.

There was a further interruption. This time it was Diggy Smith at the kitchen door. He was a stout young man, the buttons on his waistcoat straining to burst off, but he had a round pleasant face, framed by side-whiskers and a fringe beard.

"Hello, Mary. Is your father in?"

"I'm afraid not Diggy," I replied. "He's gone to Atherstone and won't be back until later."

"Will you tell him I've been, and that Doctor Jeffcoate's spoken to me about my donkeys? I'll pay your father for grazing. It seems I ain't got a leg to stand on. It's a mystery to me how they get out, honest, I keep that fence in good repair, but they're cunning little devils and they can always find a weak spot. I never done it deliberate, honest."

His face had such an expression of innocence I found myself saying, "Of course you didn't, Diggy."

"What I want to know is," he

continued, "can I have six months to pay? I'm a bit skint at the moment."

"I'll ask Father when he comes in."

I closed the door.

"Poor Diggy. He sounds very hard up."

Effie laughed. "He's always like that." She tasted the contents of the cooking-pot over the fire with a large spoon and smacked her lips. "You'll be lucky to get anything out of him at all. Tight as a drum he is, with money."

She moved to the table and started chopping herbs.

"How did you get on at the castle this morning?"

"I saw Robert Drew and he asked me for my assurance that I would continue the music lessons for at least a year."

"My! That is good!" she exclaimed.

Suddenly I remembered the letter Aunt Grace had given me from Charles. I had to be alone to read it. Making an excuse to Effie, I made my way up to the storage-room on the third floor, and as usual found it almost full of sacks—some containing grain awaiting grinding, and others flour awaiting collection.

I walked across the room and sat on a sack of grain before the dormer window in the sloping ceiling. I liked it up here. When I was a child and wanted to be alone in a make-believe world, this is where I came. From the floor below came the muffled sounds of machinery, and periodically there was the rattle of the internal hoist when Hugh sent up a sack to the grinding-room. I would not be disturbed; sacks for the day's work were taken down early each morning.

I opened Charles' letter. I did not know what to expect, but certainly not this. The words seemed to jump from the page:

> You're a cruel woman, Mary Dordon. You break my heart, and then reject me. I never want to see you again. You have made me the most miserable man in the world.
>
> I am leaving Golding Castle immediately. My presence here having become

pointless since you informed me our friendship must end.

Charles

My eyes filled with tears. I was cruel? He was cruel, trying to twist me into submission. He was the most selfish, arrogant man I had had the misfortune to meet. The only proposition such a man could put to a woman in my position was to be his mistress.

I was not his social equal. The gap was too wide, and there was no bridge to cross.

Drying my tears, I went downstairs. It was a hard world, I thought, and it made me angry. The kitchen was empty, and I looked for something to do, for I knew that if I did not keep myself occupied, I would collapse in weeping.

Picking up the basket, I went out to look for eggs. I knew all the laying places; a corner of an empty stable, the back of the cart-shed, and the lean-to adjoining the byre where Christmas kept the plough. There weren't many eggs today, and placing those I found carefully in the basket I was on my way back to the kitchen when I saw Effie coming down the path from the orchard carrying a basket of apples.

"I just went to collect the last of the apples," she explained as she approached. "I know we have such a lot already, but I do hate to see them wasted. I thought perhaps Christmas might like to take them home, with a bit of pork," she added with a blush. "Mr. Hastilow called," she continued as we walked along. "When you were upstairs—he's just got back. He says he's calling for us tonight. Wants us all to go with him to the supper in his trap. Isn't that nice of him? Mary—he's courting you all over again. I know you don't care for him, but remember he's half a gentleman."

"You mean half a gentleman is better than none." I could not control the sharpness in my voice.

"Oh, Mary, you know I didn't mean that."

"I'm sorry, Effie, but I'm feeling upset."

We entered the kitchen, and I put the basket of eggs upon the table.

"Why don't you tell me all about it," she said sympathetically.

So I sat on the stool before the fire and told Effie everything. I suppose pride had prevented me from telling her before. Now I did not care.

"I felt so afraid when you went to Birmingham, but you wouldn't listen to any of us. But no harm's done."

No harm? How little Effie knew.

"Let's think about tonight. What are you going to wear?"

"My green muslin," I replied without any enthusiasm. "What are you going to wear, Effie."

"I don't know. I haven't anything really smart enough for the castle."

"What about your brown cambric?"

"The collar and cuffs are shabby."

We discussed the gown at length, and finally decided I should improve it by sewing a piece of lace at the neck and wrists.

I sat by the window in the parlour working on Effie's gown. The work was doubly hard because Charles' letter had made me feel quite ill, and attending the Tenants' Supper with Mr. Hastilow was the last thing I wanted. I dreaded the forthcoming evening. The forced conversations, the embarrassed silences.

When the sun started to sink into the western sky I heard the wheel stop, then a short while later Father walked into the parlour. He did not sit down on the settle, nor light his customary evening pipe. Hugh passed the window and waved, and I watched him cross the footbridge and start the hill.

"Not happy, Father?"

He shook his head.

"Who could have done it, Mary? I've wracked my brains until I'm weary."

"At present no one knows, Father. The matter is in the hands of Sir Francis, and he's a very capable magistrate. Anyway, it's the Tenants' Supper tonight, and you always enjoy it."

"I don't feel like going, Mary."

"You'll enjoy it when you're there. In the meantime, why don't you do a bit of carving? I presume you intend giving it to Aunt Grace for Christmas?"

"I do. Good heavens, that's next month."

He went to the dresser and brought out the wooden board on which he worked, the half-finished swallow, and Effie's knife.

"I hope you get your knife back from Hopper." I said, but there was no reply. Father's thoughts were far away as his knife chipped away at the wood. A warm look came in his eyes. He was no longer a miller, but an artist, creating beauty where there had been none before. Christmas came in carrying two pails of milk and took them through to the dairy. I blinked in astonishment. He had now cleaned his boots and brushed his hair.

"How are you getting on?" asked

Father solicitously as Christmas came out of the dairy.

"Getting on all right, Mr. Dordon," he replied. "Ain't touched a drop for twenty-four hours. It's Effie what's done it. Nothing like having a good woman taking a fancy to you."

As he left the room Father's mouth opened in amazement.

"Effie and Christmas! What's the world coming to?"

I bent my head, suppressing a smile, and put the last stitch in her gown.

"Your gown's finished, Effie," I called, holding it up.

She hurried in, casting an embarrassed look in Father's direction.

"Oh, Mary, you have done it well. That bit of lace makes all the difference."

She took the gown from me, then turned to Father.

"Mr. Dordon, about the milk Christmas has just put in the dairy—I could make a bit of butter for you tomorrow if you like. Of course I haven't done it for years."

There was no reply from Father as his knife chipped away at the swallow's wing. It was now time to get ready, and lighting candles, Effie and I went upstairs to change, and as I dressed my thoughts turned uncomfortably to Mr. Hastilow. Effie thinks he's courting me again, but I could never marry him, not as long as I lived.

It was when I was combing my hair I remembered I had left Charles' letter in the storage-room. The embarrassment of Father or Hugh discovering it in the morning sent me hurrying up the stairs to the third floor to find it.

I opened the door, the candle-light pierced the darkness. How foolish of me to have left it here. I walked across the room to the dormer window. There was no letter to be seen. I was about to postpone the search until tomorrow's daylight, when suddenly I saw it. And as I bent down to pick it up, I saw something else—something that was so incredible, at first I thought the shadows were playing tricks, creating an optical illusion.

I looked again, and this time it was no illusion. It was real.

A hand was protruding from between the sacks.

11

FOR a few moments I seemed to be paralysed. I could neither cry, nor move, nor think. And then, mercifully, this hideous feeling left me, like a veil being lifted, and I knew what I had to do.

Pushing Charles' letter into my pocket I raised the candle and moved nervously towards the outstretched hand. The dim light of the candle revealed the body of Hopper wedged between the sacks and the wall!

He was wearing a uniform—looked like a soldier's, a red and white jacket and dark trousers, and on his beltplate I could just make out the figures "57". The 57th Foot!

Effie had been right. He had gone for a soldier. Poor dear Hopper, and now he was dead; obviously strangled, for his face was distorted and purple and his mouth open.

I found myself trembling violently. Was the murderer still in this room, I thought, lurking in the dark shadows? Perhaps he was standing behind me? I am not brave. I moved quickly in the direction of the door. To my horror I tripped over something and fell. The candle went out.

I tried to scream, but no sound came. Then I heard Effie's voice.

"Mary! You're taking a long time getting ready. It's time to be going, and Mr. Hastilow's here."

Thank heavens for Effie. I could have wept—my link with normality.

"Coming, Effie," I called back.

I fled from that room, down the stairs, along the bedroom corridor, and as I descended the second flight of stairs my thoughts became more coherent and orderly. His body must have been there this afternoon when I sat reading Charles' letter. I had noticed nothing.

Mr. Hastilow was standing by the window dressed in the blue jacket, black breeches and military long boots of the

Forest of Arden Yeomanry Cavalry—a volunteer reserve regiment that had been formed during the war years in case of invasion by Napoleon.

As I walked across the room Father was speaking to him:

"It's very good of you to go out of your way to take us tonight, Mr. Hastilow, seeing how busy you've been all week with Yeomanry matters."

I could feel Mr. Hastilow's penetrating gaze. I had never been so glad to see him.

"You look ill, Mary," he commented in his customary quiet voice.

I sank down on the settle. My legs were shaking badly.

"Hopper." I gasped. "He's in the storage-room—I think he's been strangled."

I felt I was going to faint.

"Hopper—strangled!" exclaimed Father incredulously.

"Give Mary a drop of brandy," I heard Mr. Hastilow say.

Someone put a glass in my hand, and

I drank the fiery liquid. My head started to clear.

"I told you, George, you shouldn't employ that madman." For the first time I heard Mr. Hastilow's voice raised in anger. "You know he nearly killed a man last year."

"That Diggy Smith's been hanging round here today." Effie remarked, accusation in her voice. "They do say he's half gypsy."

"Who's done it is a matter for the magistrate," replied Father. "In the meantime, what do we do now?"

"I suggest we take the body to the undertakers at Golding Magna," said Mr. Hastilow. "Inform Constable Trye, and then Sir Francis."

"What do you think Mary and Effie should do?" asked Father, looking very worried. "Don't seem respectful going off to the Tenants' Supper now."

Mr. Hastilow regarded us thoughtfully for a moment.

"I think they should go," he said. "I consider it most unwise to leave them alone and unprotected whilst we're away. At least they'll be safe at the castle."

The two men disappeared upstairs.

Effie put on her cloak and sat next to me on the settle.

"It's a blessing Mr. Hastilow's here."

I nodded in agreement.

Then she looked at me. Her blue eyes behind her steel-rimmed spectacles were full of anguish. "Mary, there's evil in this mill. I've been feeling it for a long time now."

"I feel frightened, Effie. What's going to happen next? First Alice, then Rose, and now Hopper."

"Only the Lord knows that, Mary. We must pray that whoever is doing these wicked murders will be brought to justice."

We heard the slow ponderous step of the men descending the stairs with Hopper's body. I opened the front door, and the two men passed. I thought Mr. Hastilow looked particularly miserable as Effie and I followed them out into the darkness.

We set off in the mill-cart, following Mr. Hastilow's trap carrying Hopper's body.

Effie gave a wry smile and looked at me.

"Poor Mr. Hastilow. It's not to be. Well, it'll be the queerest supper I've ever been to."

I was busy thinking about Hopper. How long had his body been in the storage-room?

"If anyone had seen or heard anything suspicious they would surely have mentioned it," I remarked to Effie as we drove along. "Did you notice anything when you came down this morning?"

Effie thought for a minute.

"I got up same time as usual, soon as it got light," she replied. "Your father got up late. Bit unusual for him. He said he'd slept badly. I'm afraid Rose's murder has upset him more than he realises. Anyway, there was no problem—Hugh had got the grinding under way, so that was a relief to your father. Danny comes in very early now because he's giving Christmas a hand with the milking."

Then a disconcerting thought filled my mind.

"I respect Mr. Hastilow's opinions. I regard him as an intelligent man, and he thinks Danny murdered Hopper. What do you think, Effie?"

Effie did not answer. I continued:

"Do you remember how Danny got himself in quite a state when Nat asked him a simple question? He was still worrying about it when I saw him today."

"Mr. Hastilow could be right," she said thoughtfully. "Christmas thinks he's a murderer. I've never felt quite sure of Danny."

Mr. Hastilow's trap was now lost from view. It was a frosty starlit night, and as we trotted along the lanes I thought how much we would have enjoyed this under other circumstances. I found myself thinking of all the other nights we had gone to the Tenants' Supper at the castle. This was one we would never forget.

At the castle gates, we turned down the

drive, over the bridge that spanned the moat, and into the courtyard. Coloured lanterns had been lit, casting their lovely pools of crimson, amber, and azure light upon the cobblestones, and as a breeze sprang up the pools of light moved like dancing will-o'-the-wisps.

The courtyard was crowded with vehicles—everything from plain carts to elegant phaetons; their passengers alighting and entering the castle by the main door. Such bustle, such activity. The mood was infectious—even Effie and I caught a little of it, despite our sombre mood. We smiled to each other.

The room set aside for the Tenants' Annual Supper was situated off the kitchen corridor, the Drews deeming such an event did not warrant the use of the great hall. Plain and bare, the walls unadorned with paintings, the windows devoid of curtains. It was also the room in which rents were paid, repairs discussed, and any other dealings a tenant may have with Sir Francis. The furniture too was simple, comprising a long trestle-table covered in a plain white cloth down the centre of the room, benches on each side; with the table for the Drews running across the top.

The room was crowded, and there was the usual buzz of excited conversation. Everybody was there: the Newcombes, the Burbiges, the Okeovers, the Purefoys, the Dunckleys. They stood about in small groups, their prosperity reflected in their fashionable clothes—the women in their loose, high-waisted robes of spotted cambric and embroidered poplin, the men in pale-coloured trousers and dark frockcoats.

Effie disappeared amongst the crowd, and I caught a glimpse of Aunt Grace, flushed and anxious. Mrs. Burbige caught my eye, waved, and moved across, expressing surprise at my sudden return, and commiserating over the death of Rose.

"I feel quite nervous now at night, even when Mr. Burbige is with me. I wish they'd hurry up and catch the fellow, then we'll all sleep easier in our beds."

I could not speak of Hopper, not tonight at any rate. Some other time when the pain was not so new. I smiled, and waved, and then suddenly the Drews arrived—Sir Francis, short, pot-bellied, with a red face surrounded by white side-whiskers, Lady Eleanor at his side, looking very regal in purple satin. Robert Drew smiled at me as he passed, and behind him came Emma, very lovely in a pale-blue creation trimmed with a great deal of lace. She was accompanied by a tall, distingnished-looking man.

I managed to catch Lady Eleanor's attention, and with profuse apologies explained that my father and Mr. Hastilow had been delayed on urgent business with Constable Trye and hoped to arrive later to discuss the matter with Sir Francis.

"My dear, I hope it's nothing serious."

"I'm afraid it is. Hopper—he's one of the men who worked for my father at the mill. He's been found murdered."

Lady Eleanor paled.

"Murdered? I don't understand. First your dairymaid and now one of the men."

She moved away and whispered to Sir Francis, who in turn stared at me so hard I felt embarrassed.

Conversation ceased as the Drew family took their places at the top table, and we moved to ours at the long trestle-table. There was a brief silence whilst Sir Francis said grace, and then with a scraping of benches on the tiled floor we sat down.

The castle maids, trim figures in their mauve gowns, starched white aprons and caps, brought in the first course, a delicious game soup. Ale was poured and handed round.

I found myself seated next to Kate Purefoy. She had been a fellow pupil at Miss Digbeth's for a while, and now a bride of one year, her swollen figure proclaimed to the world her first child would soon be born.

"How are you feeling, Kate?"

"In the best of health. Won't be long now." She gave me an eager smile. "It is nice to see you again. You'll have to tell me all about Birmingham."

I did not feel like discussing Birmingham, and before I could change the subject she did it for me.

"We're doubling the wheat next year, Mary," she bubbled on. "Prices are high, and Jack says they'll keep on rising."

I always liked Kate's cheerful outlook, and tonight I particularly appreciated it. "That man with Emma Drew is William Baddesley," she continued. "Looks serious, doesn't it? I love weddings." Then she lowered her voice to a confidential whisper. "You made a big mistake turning down Mr. Hastilow. You won't do better than him."

"When I'm an old maid I shall probably regret it."

Kate laughed.

"You won't be an old maid." She squeezed my hand. "I'm glad you're back. Just like old times. By the way, where is Mr. Hastilow?"

"He and Father are coming later."

I could not talk of murder to Kate, not tonight.

It was an excellent meal. The game soup was followed by goose, then pheasant, Windsor pudding, and finally fruit jellies and cream. Kate ate enough for two, whilst I had little appetite. The tragedies of Rose and Hopper were still too close.

Mrs. Dagley stood up at the end of the table, a trifle unsteady, her face flushed, her eyes too bright. She held up her tankard for the umpteenth helping of ale.

"Well, here today, gone tomorrow. Be merry while you can, I always says."

I looked away. Sometimes I found it hard to be civil to that woman.

"Effie told me the sad news," whispered Kate. "I guessed you didn't want to talk about it, but I felt I just wanted to say how sorry I am, Mary. Any idea who did it?"

"I'm afraid not."

"None of the murders make sense." Then Kate lowered her voice to a bare whisper. "I'm suspicious about him."

And she nodded in the direction of Sir Francis. "He's got many a maid into trouble. It was always hushed up and the girl paid off."

Just then Sir Francis rose to his feet to make his annual speech. The hub of conversation died down as he began:

"It is always a great pleasure for my family and I to meet you once a year at our annual gathering."

He beamed artificially round the room.

"And particularly so this year with the magnificent harvest we have had in this part of the country."

While Sir Francis' voice droned on, Kate's remarks had set me thinking. Was it Sir Francis who was reading the books about the Druids, and his twisted mind had become so morbidly fascinated by the subject, that he had actually decided to follow the ancient custom of offering up a sacrifice and had murdered the two girls? It was a horrific thought. The respectable magistrate was in an excellent position for covering up his crimes.

Then I remembered with a shock Rose

had worked here in the castle before she came to us. She had never given a convincing reason for leaving. Had the reason been Sir Francis?

I suddenly realised he had stopped speaking and was looking across at the door. Aunt Grace was standing there, a cloak around her shoulders, looking most agitated. He barked at her in an irritated tone:

"Yes, Mrs. Allen, what is it?"

"I'm so sorry, Sir Francis, but something terrible has happened, and what with this murderer at large I thought you'd better know straight away, because you never know what might have happened."

"Come to the point woman," he snapped impatiently.

"It's Miss Caroline. She's missing. We've searched the castle, and the grounds, and she's not here."

Robert Drew stood up, the colour drained from his face.

"You mean my daughter's run away?"

"It looks like it, sir," Aunt Grace replied.

There was a moment's silence, and then a babel of conversation broke out.

This morning Caroline had confided to me she wanted to run away. I had not taken it seriously. Not realised the depth of her unhappiness, and done nothing about it. I felt so angry with myself.

Robert Drew conferred for a few moments with his parents and then raised his hands for silence.

"Due to recent events, we are of the opinion a search must be made for Caroline immediately. Any volunteers?"

There was a show of hands, mainly from the men. I raised my hand.

Effie frowned at me from further down the table.

"Thank you. I'm very grateful," continued Robert Drew. "Not a very nice way to end an Annual supper I'm afraid. My mother thinks we ought to search the wood first. Caroline was very fond of walking in there with her brother and governess."

There was a scraping of feet and benches as the volunteers rose to their feet. I stood up with them.

"You don't have to go, Mary!" exclaimed Kate. "Leave it to the men."

"I have to go, Kate. You see, she told me she was going to run away and I did nothing about it."

12

"COLLECT lanterns at the stables," called Robert Drew as he hurried from the room.

I went into the passage outside and took my cloak from the peg.

"You'll ruin that pretty gown in Golding Wood," commented a voice behind me.

I turned round to find Jack Purefoy, Kate's husband, looking at me in a bemused way. "Stay here with Kate and the rest of the womenfolk."

"I'm coming with you, Jack," I said firmly. "I have my reasons."

We went out into the frosty night air. There must have been about ten of us. Robert Drew, now no longer the easy-going, smiling man, led the way to the stables and supervised the lighting and distribution of the lanterns.

We set off down the drive. Father and

Mr. Hastilow were a long time at the village, I thought. What was keeping them? We reached the gates, and across the lane lay the sprawling black shadow of Golding Wood.

We plunged into the trees, fanning out in a long line—the lanterns moving, dancing lights amongst the trees.

"Caroline!" called the anguished voice of Robert Drew, and the call was echoed by everyone of us.

Then we paused to listen for an answer, but none came. Only a rustle in the undergrowth as a frightened hare bounded away on its long hind legs.

We moved on. Wet autumn leaves squelching underfoot, thorns pulling at our clothes, and all the time calling for Caroline. Somewhere in the darkness an owl hooted.

We stumbled over half-hidden tree-roots, down into unexpected hollows, pushed aside branches that tried to bar our way, and at each step fear grew in our hearts. Please God, I whispered, let her be safe. Not Caroline, dear little

Caroline. Let me see that sweet face again.

"Look!" someone shouted.

Ahead of us a solitary lantern bobbed through the trees. It was moving towards us.

Robert Drew cupped his hand to his mouth.

"Hello there," he shouted.

The lantern stopped for a moment, and a man's voice called back, "Hello." Then the lantern started moving towards us again. We stopped and waited for his approach. Who was wandering in Golding Wood at this time of night?

"Bit cold for courting," commented Arthur Newcombe, blowing on his hands.

As the lantern drew near, to my astonishment its light revealed Nicholas Jeffcoate! He smiled nonchalantly at us.

"Good evening, everyone. Bit late for beagling?"

"We're not beagling," replied Robert Drew testily. "And may I ask what you are doing here?"

"That is my own concern, Mr. Drew."

"I'm afraid it is not. My daughter is missing, and I demand an explanation as to why you are in these woods at this late hour."

Nicholas gave an easy laugh.

"I'm sorry, but I can't. Not at present at any rate."

"You don't seem to understand the seriousness of the situation," Robert Drew raised his voice.

"Mr. Drew, I sincerely hope your daughter is found, but I can assure you I have nothing to do with her disappearance. In the meantime I maintain I cannot disclose why I am in this wood."

And with that he walked on. We stood speechless, watching him disappear through the trees. Robert Drew beat his fist against his palm.

"I swear I'll have him before the bench at the next assizes."

Ben Burbige gave a low whistle between his teeth.

"Whichever way you look at it, Mr. Drew, that new doctor is acting in a very queer way."

"Queer's the word for it all right," said Jack Purefoy. "You should have seen him last summer with his net. What normal man hunts butterflies?"

Everyone agreed, and we moved on. Any solitary man wandering in these woods who would not account for his actions must come under suspicion. Nicholas' behaviour puzzled me. He must know that by not answering Robert Drew's question he had placed himself in jeopardy. Why had he done it?

We seemed to have been walking for a very long time. I was now on the edge of the line, getting tired, and walking slower than the rest, so that the gap between us was gradually widening.

It did not worry me. I could see their lanterns glowing in the darkness. Then it all happened so suddenly. I caught my foot in a rabbit-hole and down I went. I must have knocked my head against a tree because I was dazed for a few minutes, and when I came to I was alone in the wood.

To make matters worse my lantern had

gone out. I struggled to my feet, calling for the searchers. But no answer came, and no friendly light pierced the darkness. After a while I stopped shouting. I have never known such a deep silence, and as I stood there the darkness seemed to be crowding in; taking shape, moving, dissolving and reforming.

I started to move, stumbling blindly through the trees, a nightmare fear I would never find the searchers. After a while I thought I saw the stars through the trees. It must be a mirage I told myself. I continued on, but the trees were thinning out! And then to my great joy I was standing on the edge of the wood, and there before me, silvered with frost, was Mozey's Meadow and Scott's Rough, sloping down to the mill.

Suddenly a gust of wind sent something flapping at my side. I turned and looked. It was a small scrap of material caught on a bramble-bush. Could it be from Caroline's gown? I pushed it into the pocket of my cloak.

Then I ran down the slope, the grass

soft beneath my feet, and overhead a black canopy glittering with stars—such a sense of release, of exhilaration.

I reached the mill, and felt along the wall until I came to the loose stone where the key was hidden. It turned stiffly in the big old lock, and I walked into the silent mill.

The fire in the parlour was almost out, and giving the dying embers a stir I put on a couple of logs and worked the bellows for a few minutes. Very soon there was a good fire blazing.

What a dreadful state I was in. My feet wet through, and my cloak torn and covered in mud. I took it off and hung it up, slipped out of my wet shoes, and peeled off my stockings. Then I looked at my muslin gown. There were a few rips in it. It could be repaired, but I would never again wear it at the castle.

Such a relief to be home. I sat down on the settle to await Father and Effie's return, watching the tongues of flame leaping around the logs. I smiled wryly to myself. I had not been much help looking for Caroline. Harry would have laughed. "You were afraid of the darkness in the wood;" he would have said, and then he would have teased me.

I must have fallen asleep, because I remember waking with a start and having the sensation I was not alone. I felt someone was watching me, and I was suddenly conscious of the intense stillness within the mill.

Then I saw the face. It was at the window, and for a moment I could not make out who it was. The man was holding a lantern in such a way it caused a distortion to his features. I felt goose-pimples creep along my arms. Then he moved the lantern and waved.

How foolish of me! It was only Hugh!

I jumped up and opened the door.

"You gave me quite a start, Hugh," I laughed. "I couldn't think who it was."

He walked past me and into the parlour, putting his lantern on the table.

"I didn't expect to see you here, Mary. I thought everyone had gone to the

Tenants' Supper. Mr. Dordon said you would not be home until very late."

Then he caught sight of the rips in my gown.

"What have you been up to? And you have mud on your face. I thought these Tenants' Suppers were supposed to be very dull affairs."

"It's nothing to joke about, Hugh. Caroline Drew is missing, and a party of us went off into the wood to search for her. I got separated and decided to come home. After two murders in that wood I wasn't feeling very brave."

"Of course not. Will your father be home soon?"

"I hope so. Oh, Hugh, you don't know the latest. I found Hopper in the storage-room. He'd been strangled. Father and Mr. Hastilow took his body to the village. They'll be seeing Constable Trye and then Sir Francis—I don't know how long that will take. It made me feel ill. Anyway, I hope Caroline is found."

"Of course she'll be found. She was probably inside the castle all the time."

"I'm not so sure," I said, walking to the dairy passage and taking the scrap of material from my cloak pocket. "I found this on a bramble-bush. It's probably from Caroline's gown."

I held it close to the lantern for Hugh to see.

"That's from Rose's gown," he said quickly.

Of course it was! It was ribbed pink silk! On Tuesday afternoon she had told me she was going to wear it.

"How did you know it was from Rose's gown? She had never worn it before."

He did not answer, and in his silence I knew the nightmare truth. I felt a wave of nausea as I moved away from him round the table.

"You lied when you told Constable Trye you hadn't seen Rose that evening."

He had the sheepish look of a schoolboy caught stealing apples.

"Why did you murder Rose?"

A hot look came into his eyes.

"I had to."

The front door was behind him, and on

the table lay the key. I watched his hand close over it. Then turning quickly he locked the door, and faced me.

"What did you mean you had to," I exclaimed. "Rose had done you no harm. Why choose her?"

"The gods want youth and innocence."

He was obviously mad!

I felt incredibly calm. I think it was because everything seemed unreal, almost theatrical, like the play I had once seen in Birmingham with Mrs. Field.

"And you told Rose to keep the friendship secret?"

"Naturally."

"I suppose you murdered Hopper as well?"

He nodded.

"And Alice?"

Again he nodded.

"They will live again in another life."

I put my hand on the table to steady myself.

"Am I talking to the same kind man who helps my father in the mill, who plays the harp, and sings beautiful Welsh ballads?"

"You are." He seemed proud of himself. "I'm very fond of those ballads. They go back to the beginning of our history. Long before the Romans came. There's a ballad too about Chyndonax."

"Who is Chyndonax?"

"He was an Arch Druid. One of the great priests." He seemed exasperated I did not know. "I'm a direct descendant of him. My real name is Chyndonax Morganwy." On his finger the ring with the letters "CM" engraved upon it shone in the lantern-light. "The Morganwys never accepted christianity," he continued. "We always kept to the old ways."

"The old ways," I repeated, feeling bewildered, and then suddenly I remembered the books in Golding Castle library, and the one that mentioned Celtic feast days when victims were sacrificed. The pattern was taking shape.

"Are you a—a Druid?"

"Of course."

And his eyes burned like someone with a fever.

I started incredulously at this strange man across the table.

"How was it possible to keep to the old ways in a christian country?" My voice was almost a whisper.

"I've told you the Morganwys have always lived in a remote part of the Black Mountains," he replied. "We kept away from people. Up there on top of Ddu Sion it was our kingdom. I've always been alone. My mother died when I was born, and I was the only child. My father was my world. He taught me to play the harp and told me about the time when the world was young. He taught me everything I know.

"When he died, for a long time I was very unhappy and confused. I did not know what to do. My world had collapsed. One day I went up to the mountaintop and prayed to Jupiter. He spoke to me. He told me I must leave my home and journey far away. He said he would give me a sign. So I put all my worldly possessions into the old cart and set off. I did not know where I was going. I was a lost soul, until the day I stopped at your mill to buy some flour. It was the day the pig had got into the cellar. I went down and helped Effie get her out, and in your cellar I saw the sign."

"In our cellar?"

There was derision in my voice.

"Yes. I saw the statue of Dis."

"Dis?"

"The god of the Under-Earth."

"We call him 'the old man of the mill'. Father's going to sell it."

Hugh was not listening.

"You see, Mary," he continued, "your father told me it was found in the foundations, so it is obvious this mill was built on the site of a long-lost Druid temple. Sacred ground had been desecrated, and Jupiter wanted me to reclaim it."

There was excitement in his face, and he was breathing rapidly.

"Your father gave me a job. But I had to wait until my chance came, and it came when he was taken ill. I discovered by chance he had not made a will, and he could not read or write. I persuaded him to make his will. He dictated it and I wrote it down, substituting my name for your brother's."

"That was wicked to disinherit Harry. How could you take advantage of an old sick man who had shown you nothing but kindness."

"He was defiling sacred ground."

If only he and Effie would come home soon, I thought desperately. How much longer could I keep him talking?

"How did you manage to persuade Rose to become a sacrifice?"

"That was easy. She was in love with me. She did everything I said. She thought it was a game."

Poor, innocent Rose. So this was her gentleman. She would have been impressed by the sheep farm he owned in Wales and his musical talent, swept along on a wave of adulation—she must have been easy.

"There's something I don't understand. On Tuesday evening we were at your cottage. You did not go to the barn dance."

He gave a cunning smile.

"I had carefully arranged to meet Rose at eleven o'clock on the turnpike. That is why I invited you to my home that evening. You were my alibi—I knew your father would leave early, and that would leave me time to meet Rose."

"I suppose the same thing happened to Alice. You took her to the wood and persuaded her to play a game?"

"Yes, but you must realise I had to do it. I had to give thanks to the gods for finding the statue of Dis. The gods demand life."

The room was warm, yet I found myself shivering. Had Effie locked the dairy door? I could not remember. The kitchen door would be locked and bolted.

"What about Hopper—why did you kill him?"

"Hopper was different. I had to kill him because he knew too much. He came to the mill this morning. It was very early. It was fortunate your father overslept and Danny was in the byre, so we were alone. I met him outside and he came into the weighing-room. He told me on Tuesday night he had followed Rose from the dance and saw us meet. He had suspected all along I was her lover, and he was so upset he decided to run away and join the army.

On Thursday night he heard Rose had been murdered, and deserted from his regiment. He accused me of killing her, and said he would go to the constable and tell everything he knew.

I had no alternative but to kill him. I didn't want to because I liked Hopper. Then I had to hide him quickly, so I took him up to the storage-room, with the intention of coming back tonight and throwing his body in the mill-pond to make it look like suicide."

"You came on a wasted journey."

"Not entirely," he said, giving an enigmatic kind of smile. From his pocket he brought out a bottle of wine and placed it on the table.

"When your father arrives, I'm going to ask him to have a drink with me. Let's be civilised about these matters."

I looked at the rich dark red liquid in the bottle. It was Spanish and expensive.

"You've poisoned that wine. I suppose it was you who stole Christmas' arsenic."

"You are an astute young woman. And I suppose you have considered that Effie would think your father had the fever again. Anyway, the dosage is very strong and the end would come quickly."

"And you would inherit the mill?"

"Precisely. The time is ripe. The gods have been appeased."

"And what will you do when you've got the mill?"

"Pull it down and rebuild the temple in all its former glory, and once again the true gods will be worshipped—they've been neglected long enough."

I felt I could not stand the ravings of his poor, sick, twisted mind much longer.

"You've thought of everything," I said with sarcasm in my voice.

"I certainly have," he replied with a

slow smile. "Except for one thing. I hadn't really planned it but now I have no alternative. You now know too much, and that is dangerous. I'm going to kill you."

13

THE blood was pounding in my ears like the roar of the sea as we stared at each other across the table. The lantern-light gave his face a strange, unearthly quality. It cannot be true I kept thinking. This Welshman with his charm, his lilting musical voice, who played the harp like an angel, so kind and helpful to my father—a vile, insane killer.

How wrong we can be about our fellow human beings. The careful cunning facade that is paraded before the world, whilst the real person is kept hidden in deep depths, that is, until the day he betrays himself.

Hugh had betrayed himself tonight. A chance slip of the tongue in an over-confident moment. But for that my father too would have been found dead.

"I had other plans for you," Hugh was saying, and the look in his eyes was now almost sickly sentimental. "I like you, Mary. I like you a lot. You're my kind of woman. Got plenty of spirit."

"How do you propose to kill me?" I asked in a voice that sounded hoarse and unnatural.

He brought the knife from his pocket —the cold steel glinting in the lantern-light.

Another sacrifice, I thought. I, too, would end up like Rose and Alice, covered in oak leaves and holding a posy of flowers in Golding Wood.

Then suddenly I was blazing mad—a red-headed Dordon does not give in easily. With a quick movement I picked up the bottle of wine and threw it at him. It missed and hit the wall, shattering into fragments, the poisonous red liquid staining the white wall.

Hugh raised his knife and lunged forward across the table as I picked up the lantern and hurled it at him.

Suddenly Nat Trye was standing in the kitchen doorway.

"Get out of the way, Mary," he shouted.

As he rushed forward to tackle Hugh, a tongue of flame from the broken lantern was already devouring the curtains. I ran into the weighing-room and closed the door, leaning breathlessly against it, listening. It was over very quickly. A quick scuffle, the table overturned, then there was a groan and a thud. I could take no chances. I needed to wedge the door, but there were only sacks of grain and they would take too long to drag across the floor.

There was still the outside door of the weighing-room. I ran to it and turned the handle, but to my intense disappointment it was locked.

The pale starlight from the little window showed me the ladder at the rear of the room leading up to the grinding-room.

As I ran across the room I heard the parlour door open, and as I started to climb the ladder footsteps sounded on the stone floor. I knew from the quick sound it was Hugh. My long gown was hindering my ascent, and then to my horror as I approached the top I felt him catch the hem and pull.

I held onto the ladder with all my strength, my body in a glow of nervous perspiration. Thank heaven it was only thin muslin, already weakened by the thorns of Golding Wood. I heard the tear as a section came away in his hand, and freed from his restraint I raced the last few steps.

"You won't get away," he called.

There was a sack of flour about a foot from the top of the ladder leaning against the wall, and a second one a few feet away. Hugh was half-way up the ladder. I pushed the sack down the ladder; the contents, about half a hundredweight of flour, hit him in the face, and giving a cry of rage, he fell to the bottom.

There was not a moment to lose. Whilst Hugh lay at the bottom of the ladder, spitting flour from his mouth, and rubbing it from his eyes, sweating and panting I dragged the second sack to the top of the ladder and waited for him.

After a few moments he stood up, a grotesque, evil figure white with flour.

"You're wasting your time, Mary," he called, as he started to mount the ladder.

My heart thumping against my ribs, I waited until he was about half-way up, and then I tipped the contents of the second sack over him. This time he held the ladder so securely he did not lose his balance. But the flour again momentarily blinded him, and he had to pause on the ladder to rub it from his eyes.

Smoke was now billowing from the parlour in an alarming way. Was Nat lying dead in there?

There were no more sacks. I ran into the darkness of the grinding-room like a frightened animal cornered in the chase, crouching behind the grinding stones, trembling and sick with fear.

He was a strong man and could easily overpower me. Only my wit could save me now. But what could I do?

The grinding stones were the only big

structure in the room, and it was obvious I would hide behind them. He would make straight for them. There would be a cat-and-mouse chase in the dark, and it would only be a matter of time.

Then suddenly out of my anguish an idea was born. The internal hoist lay directly between the grinding stones and the top of the ladder. When Father finished work each evening the trap-doors surrounding the hoist were always closed. His habit never varied, and each morning he would draw back the bolts and let the flaps drop.

I crawled towards it in the smoky darkness. I knew from habit its exact position. There was a small gap where the actual chain went through the floor. Quick as a flash I put my hand down, slid back the bars and the trap-door flaps fell inwards. As I scurried back to my hiding-place behind the grinding stones Hugh's head and shoulders appeared in the ladder opening smoke swirling about him.

He stepped onto the grinding-room floor and paused, breathing deeply like an animal gathering strength for the attack. A pale glow from below lit his figure in a dark silhouette. Then he moved foward towards the grinding stones.

An itching sensation had started in my throat and I desperatedly wanted to cough. So putting my hand over my mouth I took a deep breath and held it, and as I did so I willed him to walk across the open trapdoor.

But there was no need. As I heard his cry I closed my eyes and prayed. Then there was the thud of his body as it hit the stone floor of the weighing-room below.

I burst into a fit of coughing, and when my throat was relieved I pressed my cheek against the old wooden floor and wept.

After a while my sobbing subsided, and I lay there unmoving, feeling quite weak. Then gradually I became conscious of heat from below—the floorboards were becoming uncomfortably hot, and the glow in the ladder opening had increased so that the grinding-room was now partially lit.

I stood up, half dazed, my bare feet painful on the hot wooden floor. I could now hear the roar of flames below, then the ominous crack as a roof support in the weighing-room collapsed.

Then to my horror the ladder ignited, and a burst of flame leapt in the ladder opening. I was now terror-stricken, and ran to the end of the room, up the ladder to the storage-room, standing for a few minutes in the hot darkness, panting for breath, the sacks around me warm to the touch.

I had been saved from a maniac killer, to be burnt alive in the mill!

There was a window here, but I was now on the third floor, and jumping from such a height would probably end in my death.

The mill-pond!

Why hadn't I thought of it before. Father's bedroom was on the floor below, and situated at the rear of the house. There was a chance, and my spirits rose. I retraced my steps down the ladder.

In the grinding-room the flames were

licking around the hoist, and the atmosphere was filled with the smell of roasting grain combined with the stinging smell of smoke. Coughing, my eyes watering, I opened the door leading to our private quarters. Here was the bedroom corridor, and the staircase leading down to the parlour was a raging torrent of flames. I ran the few feet across the landing and opened father's door, the wood hot to my touch, the paint blistering, and closed the door.

The room was full of smoke. I started coughing and could not stop. Outside on the landing a large piece of timber crashed, partly piercing the door, and tiny fingers of flame crept stealthily around the edge of the door.

I was trapped!

The heat was unbearable. As a sensation of dizziness overcame me I sat down on Father's bed. The room was slowly moving.

The window! I must get to the window! I staggered across the room colliding with furniture. The window opened by sliding sideways. Father rarely opened it, consequently I found it stiff to the touch. My hands, wet with perspiration pushed.

It would not move!

But I must open it, I thought desperately. Coughing, my eyes still streaming, I pushed again—this time with every ounce of strength I possessed. It started to move, and I kept on pushing until it was completely back, then leaning out I gulped in the fresh night air. The relief was enormous.

The cold fresh air cleared my head, and I brushed the tears from my eyes with the back of my hand. The smooth surface of the mill-pond was stained crimson from the glow of the flames. It was tantalisingly near but just too far to jump.

But what was happening? There were people on the far side. They were passing buckets, the light from the fire paling their faces.

I shouted and waved like someone demented. Then a breeze blew wreaths of smoke around them, and I could see them no more.

There was a sudden crackling behind me. I turned to find the draught from the window had fanned the few flames around the door into a curtain of fire. The heat and smoke was intense.

I remember a crashing sound; then a spinning, falling sensation; then darkness.

14

THE sound of church bells floated through my dreams. Such a tranquil sound, full of peace and serenity, and childhood memories. I stretched, and lazily opened my eyes.

I was in a strange room! The walls were covered in paper painted with flowers and birds, and I was lying in a grand four-poster bed. The cover was of the finest damask. I touched it; my fingers moving gently over the smooth, silky surface. I had never know such luxury.

A fire burned in an elegant grate, and on the mantelpiece a small jade clock gently ticked away. To the left of the bed was a graceful dressing-table, on the top of which lay silver-backed hair-brushes and a small hand mirror, and to the right a mahogany washstand, the top inlaid with marble, bearing a large jug and bowl, and a freshly laundered white towel.

Where was I? I had no recollection of ever having been in such a room. Then I looked down at my hands. There was a burn mark on the right hand.

The mill! And all the horror of it came back with such a force I could almost feel the heat and the fear all over again. I tried to sit up, but a thumping pain in my head made me lie back again on the pillows.

I must have dozed off, for I awoke to see the familiar figure of Aunt Grace bending over me. Of course, I should have realised I was in Golding Castle—the only house in the district that possessed such opulent rooms. Aunt Grace, wearing her Sunday-best cap and apron, gave me a kiss on the cheek.

"How are you feeling, Mary?"

I smiled. "I feel hungry."

"That's a good sign. My, how you've slept. You've slept the clock round twice over and more. Sleep's better than any doctor's medicine. Speaking of doctors, he said he was coming this morning to have a look at you."

"Today must be Sunday. I heard the church bells ringing."

"It's Sunday all right, and they're all at church, that is except Sir Francis. Now, would you like a bowl of porridge with a bit of honey and cream?"

"I'd like that very much, Aunt Grace. You know, you're spoiling me."

"It's a pleasure, Mary, after what you've been through."

"Why am I in Golding Castle?"

"Can't you remember anything?"

"I have a hazy memory of someone carrying me, of voices, and darkness, and a terrible pain in my head."

"I'm not surprised. You've got a lump on your head size of an egg. You must have had a terrible blow. Mr. Robert and the others brought you here, and it was Lady Eleanor, bless her, who insisted you were put in a guest-room. You'll go a long way before you find a lady as kind as her."

"I must thank her. Whose nightgown am I wearing?"

"That's one of mine. What a sight you

were. Your green muslin was in shreds, and your face was as black as a chimney sweep's. Don't worry, I gave you a good wash. Oh, Mary, I've been so worried about you, and so has your father."

"Where is he?"

"I think he's at the Wheatsheaf with Effie. I told him I could find him a bed here, but he said he wasn't going to be a trouble to anyone. You know how obstinate he can be."

"I know. Aunt Grace, who rescued me?"

"I don't know. There were such a lot of people with Mr. Robert when he brought you back. I'm talking too much. I must go and get that porridge."

And with that she hurried from the room.

It's all my fault, I thought guiltily. If I had not thrown that lantern at Hugh the mill would never have set on fire. Hugh had confessed the murders to me, and Nat Trye had obviously overheard in the kitchen, but poor Nat was now probably dead—perished in the flames. I suddenly realised I must tell Sir Francis, the sooner the better.

Within a few minutes Aunt Grace returned with a steaming bowl of porridge, a cup of tea, and a slice of bread and butter.

"Let's see you eat that," she said as she placed the tray on the bed. "And drink the tea while it's hot. I'm a great believer in tea."

I sipped the tea obediently before I spoke.

"Aunt Grace, I have something very important to tell Sir Francis about the murders."

She gave me a sharp look.

"About the murders? I'll go and tell him right away."

I had just finished eating when there was a tap at the door.

"Come in," I called, as I leaned over and put the tray on the bedside table.

The door opened and Sir Francis hobbled in on a walking-stick, each movement as he progressed across the room stiff and painful. He looked as though his maid-chasing days were over.

"Good morning, Miss Dordon," he said, easing himself into the bedside chair. He looked old, tired, and sorry for himself. How foolish of me to have thought he was the murderer. I felt embarrassed.

"How are you after your ordeal?"

"Very much better, thank you, Sir Francis."

"You're in good hands with Mrs. Allen." He stretched out his legs. "Gout's bad today, damn it. Couldn't make it to church. Not that I worry about that. We must get the worst sermons in the county. What did you want to see me about?"

"I—I want to tell you that just before the fire started Hugh Morganwy, he was employed by my father, confessed to the murders . . ."

"I know all about that," he interrupted. "Constable Trye overheard everything and told me about it yesterday."

"Constable Trye? But I thought he . . ."

"He was rescued, in the nick of time, and none the worse for it. He's given me his statement, and I would like one from you, for the Inquiry. Give it to me as soon as you can. I want to get the whole wretched business finished and done with."

"Yes, Sir Francis."

"I've seen your father. What was he doing engaging a stranger, and a Welshman at that, when there's enough unemployment in the district? Answer me that," he barked.

I remained silent not knowing what to say.

He eased himself slowly from the chair.

"Never did like the Welsh," he said irritably. "You can't trust the damn fellows. Good day to you, Miss Dordon."

He hobbled painfully from the room and closed the door. I leaned back on the pillows and breathed a sigh of relief. Thank goodness that was over. I never felt at ease in Sir Francis' company at the best of times—today had been the worst. Aunt Grace put her head round the door.

"Just looking to see if he's gone. Hope he didn't upset you."

I smiled weakly.

"Never mind. Dr. Jeffcoate wants to see you."

She opened the door further and allowed him to enter.

"Well, Mary, and how are you this morning?"

He looked very smart in his dark green frockcoat decorated with brass buttons, his top hat under his arm, and a pair of leather gloves in his hand. He gave me a solemn smile and sat down. Such a pity, I thought, that everyone regarded him as an oddity. He was really a very nice man.

"I'm feeling very much better thank you, Nicholas."

Very tenderly he felt the lump on my head.

"Still hurt?"

"Just a bit."

"How's the burn?"

"Just feels a bit uncomfortable."

"I've given Mrs. Allen instructions for the bathing of the burn and the swelling.

You've been extraordinarily lucky, Mary."

I smiled in agreement.

"Tragedy about the mill though. What do you think your father will do?"

"I don't know."

"Now, you must stay in bed for two more days. We can't be too careful. Not feeling dizzy?"

I assured him I was not. He rose to go.

"Nicholas. We've known each other a long time."

"What are you leading up to, Mary?"

He looked amused.

"Why were you so secretive in the wood on Friday night?"

"It's no secret now. I saw Sir Francis and Robert last night. I have another hobby. It's ornithology." An excited note crept into his voice. "You see, I had made a remarkable discovery—a rare species of white owl in Golding Wood. I had to keep my discovery secret until I had submitted my paper to the Royal Ornithological Association. When I met you all in the wood the other night, I was in an extremely difficult position. Anyway, I sent off my paper yesterday by the fastest mail to London, then came up here straight away to see the Drews.

"Fortunately they were most understanding about it. You see, the crisis had passed and Caroline had been found."

"Where was she?"

"It's quite ridiculous. She was asleep under her bed all the time. It was some make-believe game children play. You know the sort of thing they do. Nobody thought of looking underneath her bed. Anyway, it's all over now."

"What a relief! I'm so glad she was found. And I suppose on Tuesday night you were studying the white owl?"

He smiled, nodding. "When will you come to Atherstone?" He spoke in a quiet, self-conscious way.

"I'm not sure, Nicholas. Perhaps later."

"Next year?" He gave a sad smile. "Or never."

"Please, Nicholas . . ."

I did not want to hurt him, but it was inevitable. He put on his gloves.

"Good-bye, Mary."

There was a note of finality in his voice. As he opened the door to go Lady Eleanor was standing there with Caroline and Jamie.

"Good morning, Doctor Jeffcoate. We were just coming to see the patient. How is she?"

"Very much better, your ladyship."

He gave her a small bow before disappearing down the corridor. Lady Eleanor and the children entered the room and closed the door.

"What a dreadful business. Thank heaven you were saved, Miss Dordon." She looked very stately in an extra large poke-bonnet trimmed with ostrich feathers. "Now you must stay here as long as you wish; I insist. Mrs. Allen will get you anything you require."

"Lady Eleanor, I can't thank you enough for your kind hospitality."

"Say no more. It was the least I could do."

"I wish I'd been in the mill when it set on fire," said young Jamie, looking at me enviously.

"Be quiet, Jamie," said his grandmother. "You promised me you would be a good boy."

"I am a good boy. Look at all the trouble Caroline has caused."

"Yes, it was naughty of Caroline to fall asleep underneath her bed, and she's not going to do that again."

Caroline hid her face in the folds of her grandmother's gown.

"There, there, Caroline," soothed Lady Eleanor, patting the little girl's head. "It's all forgotten and in the past. While you're here, Miss Dordon, feel free to play the pianoforte any time you wish. It's a pleasure for me to hear it being played. Caroline practises every day, don't you, Caroline?"

Caroline smiled shyly at me.

"We'll have to be going now. Nearly time for lunch. I'm very glad to see you looking so much better."

"Thank you, Lady Eleanor."

She left the room with the two children following.

How kind and generous she was, I thought. How could I ever repay her? My thoughts were interrupted by Aunt Grace bustling in.

"My word, what a lot of visitors you're having, Mary." She picked up the tray from the bedside table. "I'm glad to see you've eaten all that porridge. I have a terrible time with those children. They're so finicky about food. Oh, I nearly forgot—your father's waiting in my sitting-room. I'll send him along right away. He's getting tired of waiting."

As she hurried from the room I thought of him. What will he do now? He was ruined. No home; no income.

"Mary!"

His voice boomed as he stood in the open doorway. He looked well rested, had taken care to brush his hair, and his side-whiskers had been trimmed. He walked across the room with a confident tread and sat down. He leaned forward and kissed me on the cheek.

"How are you feeling, Mary?"

His eyes were on my hands.

"That burn will soon heal. Grace tells me you have a lump on your head. Anyway, you were saved—that's what counts."

"Who did save me, Father?"

"I don't know who it was who went up the ladder. We didn't know you were in the mill until we saw you at the window. Thank God you're safe, Mary."

He touched my hands. His eyes watered a little, then he blew his nose very loud.

"I hear you're staying at the Wheatsheaf, Father."

"Best place round here. Old Tom Maddox does you well. Breakfast this morning were mutton chops, kidneys, and a pint of porter." He smacked his lips. "You can't do better than that. It's good of the Drews to have you, Mary. They must think a lot of you."

"How's Effie?"

"Wonders never cease. Christmas, sober as a judge, took Effie to church this morning." He shook his head in wonderment. "Well, Mary, I'm glad to see you looking so well. Healthy bloom on your cheeks already."

"Thank you, Father. You're very cheerful this morning."

"It's the only way, Mary. Put up a front to the world. Show them you don't care, but all the time you're crying inside."

I felt a lump rise in my throat.

"Oh, Father. I suppose you heard all about it from Nat. How I threw the lantern at Hugh and started the fire. It's all my fault."

Tears welled in my eyes.

"Which do you think I'd rather have?" His voice was gruff. "You dead and still have the mill? Talk sense, girl."

"Yes, Father."

"Now don't let's hear any more of that nonsense."

He walked over to the window.

"Oh, I haven't told you. Sir Francis is very kindly letting us rent one of his cottages until we get organised again. You can just see it over there through the trees." Then he turned and faced me. "Takes a long time to rebuild."

"Rebuild? Father, I don't understand. Where's the money coming from?"

"The bank's going to lend it to me, at five per cent. Golding's got to have its own mill. Why, the nearest one to here is over seven miles away. That's too far for a lot of people. Of course I'll have to pay them back as quickly as possible. There'll be lean years ahead, Mary." He braced his shoulders.

"I'll help you all I can, Father."

"You'll never guess what happened this morning," he said, his tone changing as he walked back to the bed. "It rained all last night, and I decided this morning I'd go down to the mill and have a look round—see if I could salvage anything. And who do you think I saw walking around having a nose about—Robert Drew. Anyway, I decided to have a look down the cellar—had a feeling I'd put some tools down there, and Tom Maddox had lent me a lantern.

"Robert Drew followed me down, and when he saw the old statue he seemed interested, wanted to examine it in daylight. So we lugged it out of the cellar. What a job that was. I didn't realise it was so heavy. I thought we'd never get it up the steps, and when we finally got it out, he started rubbing it with his pocket handkerchief.

"Just bronze underneath that dirt," I told him. "But he didn't take any notice of me, and after a bit he said, 'I think they're Greek letters at the base.' He seemed excited. Well, I didn't know what that signified. I thought him a bit odd. So I said, 'What does that mean?' And he said, 'This statue is very old.' I said, 'I know it is. My father found it in the foundations when we were extending the dairy.' Anyway, he said he'd like to bring it back here and examine it properly with a view to buying it. I told him I didn't mind what he did—my daughter wants me to get rid of it, anyway. So we brought it back in the mill-cart and it's in the court-yard now."

"I hope he buys it," I said.

"I don't know how much bronze is worth," said Father thoughtfully. "Might be a few guineas."

Talking about the statue brought back painful memories of Hugh.

"I suppose Nat told you Hugh confessed to the murders."

Father nodded with a grim expression on his face. "Actually Nat went to the mill looking for Danny. Lucky he went into the kitchen and overheard. I still can't believe it! Hugh of all people! It's not the man I knew. I knew a good man." He sat down on the bedside chair, an unhappy expression on his face. "Oh, Mary, it's shaken my faith in human nature. I feel I can never put my trust in anyone again."

I touched his hand.

"It will come back. Just you see."

"Perhaps. I don't know."

He rose to his feet.

"I'll have to be going. Oh, I nearly forgot. Had a letter from Harry, came yesterday. He's leaving the navy and coming home for good."

"Oh, Father, I'm so glad. Harry's company is just what you need right now. He'll give you your faith back in human nature. Any idea when he'll arrive?"

"Next week or so. Something to look forward to. Well, I've got a lot to do. We're moving into this cottage tomorrow."

He kissed me on the cheek.

"Look after yourself, Mary."

"And you, Father."

He walked across to the door.

"Oh, Father, I forgot to tell you Diggy wants six months to pay."

He stopped at the door and looked back.

"We've gone into partnership. There's money in donkeys."

I could not help smiling.

"There's another bit of good news for you. Good-bye, Mary."

He closed the door.

I lay there a long time thinking about Father, about Harry's homecoming, and then I thought about the lean years ahead. The future seemed bleak.

Then from below came the tinkling sound of childish fingers playing a nursery rhyme on the pianoforte, then Caroline's thin, clear voice singing the words: "Ring a ring a roses, a pocket full of posies . . ." Caroline at least was happy, playing a tune for her beloved Papa.

The pianoforte playing came to an end, and the room was silent once more, save for the little jade clock softly ticking away. I had the feeling my life was ticking away, unshaped, unresolved. After a while I was filled with a restlessness and sense of frustration that grew to such proportions I could bear to lie in the bed no longer. I was going to disobey Nicholas' instructions and get up.

But what could I wear? All my clothes had been burnt in the fire, and my green muslin was torn beyond repair. I leaned over and pulled the bell-rope.

I did not have to wait long. Lotty poked her head round the door and grinned at me.

"My, you look like a duchess in that bed. What do you want, your royal highness."

"I'm not in the mood for joking, Lotty. Will you tell Aunt Grace I want to get up, and I haven't anything to wear?"

"I've got a spare gown. I'll see what she says."

When Aunt Grace appeared she was carrying a lemon-coloured sarcenet gown and shawl over her arm. She lay them tenderly on the bed.

"It's very kind of you, Aunt Grace, but I would have been quite happy wearing Lotty's gown."

"I want you to wear it, Mary," she said quietly. "I think it will fit you. I was as slim as you at your age."

It was the style of twenty years ago with a bustle and small hoop. I felt puzzled, wondering why she had kept it so long, but did not comment for fear she should think me ungrateful.

"It didn't bring me any luck," she said in a wistful voice. "Might be different for you."

Then suddenly the realisation dawned on me.

"This was your wedding-gown!"

"It was, Mary. I've kept it all these years. I don't know why—it certainly doesn't have any happy memories for me. It's yours if you want it."

"Thank you, Aunt Grace. It will be an honour to wear it."

I got out of bed.

"You're going to get me into trouble with Doctor Jeffcoate," she said as she helped me into the gown. "He said you were to stay in bed another two days."

"I feel well, Aunt Grace. Really I do. The headache's almost gone."

"You're a strong girl like your mother."

She buttoned up the back.

"You'll need this warm shawl. Chilly out of the sun. Now if you start to feel ill, you get straight back into that bed."

"Yes, Aunt Grace."

Aunt Grace stepped back to survey me.

"It looks well on you, Mary. The

colour suits your hair a treat. Turn round."

As I turned there was such a wealth of material in the skirt it was a delightful sensation.

"A bit different from those skimpy gowns they wear today. I'll have to leave you, Mary, and get back."

She hurried from the room. I lingered a moment, not sure what to do, then I opened the door.

15

OUTSIDE was a long corridor, at the end of which I found a narrow, spiral of stone steps leading into the music-room. It was deserted, and the pianoforte, with the lid open, beckoned.

Like someone in a dream I walked across to it and sat down upon the little velvet stool, placed my hands on the keyboard, and started to play Charles' Brussels Sonata. I don't know why. Perhaps because it was a part of him I would always have. And as I played a sense of loss overcame me that was so powerful I had to stop.

I loved him—it was like a door opening in my mind, but instead of my heart singing I was drowning in unhappiness—it was too late.

"Why did you stop?"

I spun round. Charles was walking

towards me! I had not heard the door open, and he took me so completely by surprise I could think of nothing to say, and to make matters worse a flush was rising in my face.

He reached the pianoforte, leaned on it, giving me a hard, searching look.

His right hand was bandaged!

"It was you who saved me," I managed to say.

"It was, Mary."

"But for you . . ."

Suddenly my vision blurred, and I had to stop. He took out his pocket handkerchief and handed it to me.

"Here, Mary, dry your tears. Aren't you supposed to be in bed?"

"I've disobeyed doctor's orders. I feel so much better. I suppose you consider me a very bad patient?"

"I do."

"I hope your hand is not painful."

"Not in the least."

"I thought you were in Birmingham."

"I have my reasons for coming back."

There was an awkward pause. How

stiff the conversation was—like two strangers who had never met. I tried again.

"Will you be returning soon to your regiment?"

"In a day or so."

His tone was almost one of indifference, and it hurt. I pulled the shawl around my shoulders, and stood up.

"I think I'll go for a stroll in the sunshine."

"May I come with you?" he said, to my surprise.

"I should be delighted."

Charles opened the outer door and we walked into the courtyard. There a strange sight met our eyes. Robert Drew, my father, and William Baddesley were watching a manservant cleaning the old statue from the mill. He was working hard with a large scrubbing-brush and soap, and as he scrubbed a shining, golden surface was revealed. It glittered in the sunshine. It was quite incredible. We stood at a distance, watching, unnoticed.

"That bronze comes up nice when it's cleaned," I heard Father remark.

Robert Drew moved closer to the statue.

"It isn't bronze, Mr. Dordon," he rebuked. "It's gold!"

"Gold!" repeated Father, his voice sounding hoarse from shock. "I never knew it were gold, and neither did my father. To think that all these years . . ."

Father's problem appeared to have been solved.

Robert Drew turned to William Baddesley.

"What do you make of it, William?"

"Quite extraordinary, and it's so crude."

"It's the Greek letters that interest me," continued Robert. "The Druids used Greek. I know a bit about this sort of thing. Got interested in ancient religions when I was stationed in Egypt . . ."

We continued across the courtyard. So it was Robert Drew who was reading the books in the library! I should have guessed, and Hugh must have known the statue's value, but its religious significance was of more importance to him.

On the moat the white swans glided silently to and fro amongst the green leaves of the water-lilies.

It was very peaceful.

"Why did you run away that night?" Charles' voice was quiet and controlled. "I came to make you an honourable proposal of marriage."

"Marriage?"

"Of course."

"But I thought . . ." and then I stopped, too embarrassed to continue.

Charles' face creased into a smile.

"Mary, how could you?"

"What else was I to think? My employer's son begging for admission in the middle of the night. And I was after all only the governess."

"I never saw you as that. To me you were an intelligent, sensitive musician, and a beautiful woman. What an impetuous fool I've been! I've ruined everything. You see, that night I had just returned from a business meeting with Father and his partner. Up to that time I had only heard vague talk about setting up a factory in India, but at the meeting I discovered their plans had been finalised. Father's partner would continue the business in Birmingham, and Father was leaving at the end of November for Calcutta, taking my stepmother and the girls with him.

"I was astonished. I asked what was going to happen to you, and Father said your services would be terminated in the next week or two. The thought that I would never see you again appalled me.

"I left the meeting early and came home to think quietly, and decide what to do. I felt so depressed. Then you came in, remember? I had to kiss you. The slap you gave me only increased my ardour, and decided me what I was going to do. I was going to ask you to marry me. Once I had decided, I couldn't wait until morning. I went up to your room, but you would not open the door. It was understandable—my clumsiness downstairs had upset you, so I decided to ask you in the morning. But the next day you had gone. I was desperate to see you again. You know the rest."

"And I thought you came here to see Emma Drew."

"Whatever gave you that idea? It was always understood she would marry Baddesley."

"It doesn't matter now."

"And of course you thought you were fighting to keep a seducer at bay. What a mess I've made of everything."

We continued walking along the grassy bank of the moat.

"What made you come back, Charles?"

"Guilty conscience I suppose. I was in a temper when I wrote that letter, and I didn't mean a word I said. You see what a dreadful person I am. Inconsiderate, and bad-tempered."

"I have my faults too."

"I don't believe it."

There was a soft smile playing about his lips.

We had stopped walking. Across the

water the last of the autumn sunshine warmed and mellowed the old castle wall, and moss clung in crevices like green velvet.

"I'll never forget coming down the hill and seeing the mill a blazing inferno, and you, my precious, were in those flames."

"Yes, and alone with the murderer."

And I told him the whole story. When I finished he frowned.

"I was in Golding Wood on Tuesday night. You didn't suspect me . . ."

"Only momentarily, Charles."

His hand went round my waist.

"I should think so. By the way, I've had a reply from the music publisher. I didn't expect to hear from him so soon."

"What did he say?"

"He's going to publish the sonata, and has every hope the work will be performed in the next few months."

"Congratulations! I'm so happy."

"I'm leaving the army. Going to buy a

house in the country and concentrate on composing."

"I'm not surprised. What will you do? More sonatas?"

"I had considered it."

"Why don't you try something different. A bigger work—a pianoforte concerto for instance. You can do it. You have the talent, the maturity. There are passages in the Brussels sonata that . . ."

Then suddenly his mouth was on mine, kissing me with such passion I was left breathless, dizzy, his arms enfolding me like an iron band. I closed my eyes, and in that moment I knew true ecstasy.

"I love you so much," he whispered.

"And I love you."

"Never run away from me again."

"No, my darling, never," I breathed.

"You don't know how much I've suffered. I wanted you so much."

Then he pressed his face to my neck, his skin hot against my cool flesh.

"Marry me, Mary. I can't live without your love, your faith, your encouragement."

I had found my bridge. It had been there all the time.

THE END

Other titles in the
Linford Romance Library:

A YOUNG MAN'S FANCY
by Nancy Bell

Six people get together for reasons of their own, and the result is one of misunderstanding, suspicion and mounting tension.

THE WISDOM OF LOVE
by Janey Blair

Barbie meets Louis and receives flattering proposals, but her reawakened affection for Jonah develops into an overwhelming passion.

MIRAGE IN THE MOONLIGHT
by Mandy Brown

En route to an island to be secretary to a multi-millionaire, Heather's stubborn loyalty to her former flatmate plunges her into a grim hazard.